HELD
FOR
RANSOM

May 2001
For Maude

HELD
FOR
RANSOM

•

Terri Alcock

Wishing you all the best. Love
Terri

AVALON BOOKS
NEW YORK

PRINTED IN THE UNITED STATES OF AMERICA
ON ACID-FREE PAPER
BY HADDON CRAFTSMEN, BLOOMSBURG, PENNSYLVANIA

For my long-awaited and much loved
grandson, Alec Jordan, born
December 31, 2000

Chapter One

As I trudged up the stairs of James Bay's only commercial office building, it struck me that several months had passed since my presence had graced its shabby interior. At the top of the stairs and only a little out of breath, my heart warmed to the sight of the sign on the door. It still announced HOPE & HENRY, PRIVATE INVESTIGATORS, in impressive, though slightly tarnished, gold letters. Bill hadn't removed my name!

I pulled out the key, which I had never returned, and stuck it into the lock. Bill Henry, my old partner, and his new bride Emily, who had been *my* friend long before Bill ever met her, had left on their honeymoon a few days earlier, after a wedding that had closely missed being the social event of the sea-

1

son. Emily's parents had money, and they liked to spend it on their only daughter.

After they'd been gone for a short time, Bill had suddenly remembered that someone should be checking on things at the office—picking the mail up off the floor and retrieving messages from the answering machine. He'd called from Paris and asked me to go in and make sure all was well. Ostensibly I was tasked with the job of watering the plants and taking care of housekeeping items, but I had other plans. While Mimi, my Old English sheepdog, and I had been walking the short distance from my apartment to the office, I'd had a brilliant idea. Since these moments of sheer genius don't come along very often, I've sworn to always follow up on them and see where they lead. Usually it's right into a heap of trouble, but I have made it a policy never to let that deter me.

After giving the key a couple of jiggles, I felt the tumblers inside the lock fall into place, and the door opened in front of me. I stepped inside carefully, so as not to tread on the stack of mail that had been pushed through the slot in the door and was scattered across the floor. Mimi was not so circumspect. She left several big, muddy pawprints on an official-looking envelope, before I could grab her collar and pull her back.

Nothing had changed since my last visit. Bill had not redecorated, nor had he dusted from the look of things. As always, the place was in need of a good cleaning.

I strode over to one of the two interior doors, the one that led to my old office, opened it, and peeked inside. Other than the obvious lack of a computer on the desk—a relatively clean patch surrounded by thicker dust showed where it had once sat—the office was just the way I'd left it. Last year's calendar, the month of June still showing, hung on the wall, and a basket of flowers, which I had forgotten on the corner of the desk, had, over time, become a dried arrangement, not exactly what was intended when the flower shop across the street sent them over the previous summer.

I sat down in my old chair and was immediately engulfed in a powerful wave of nostalgia. After my investigation into the disappearance—no, murder—of the missing teenager Allison Gillespie, and having suffered through its hair-raising conclusion the previous summer, I had vowed to Bill, and to my roommate Gabby, to stay away from the sleuthing business for a while. And what's more, I had kept my word. Neither had I been gainfully employed at anything else since then, having taken advantage of the down time to write another mystery novel based on some of the events surrounding Allison's death. The book, my second, had sold well, and the proceeds, though not a fortune, had enabled me to pay my share of the household expenses in the ensuing months.

But, gosh darn it, life had been just a little too quiet for my tastes. It lacked spice, and as even those of us who don't cook know, it's the spices that make a dish. And a life!

Bill and Emily weren't expected back for months. When he'd called, I had promised to come by the office once a week, pick up and pay the bills, and answer any urgent phone messages. "And water the plants, occasionally," he had said, though I knew he didn't give a tinker's damn about them. He had simply been trying to impress Emily.

I flipped on the lights and threw my jacket onto a nearby chair. Opening the windows in the reception area and in my office to create a cross breeze and chase out the stale air, I went over to the sink and turned on the tap, leaving the water running for a while to get rid of the warm rusty liquid that had accumulated in the pipes. I filled the coffeepot, dumping the water into the electric coffee maker. There was an old rag under the sink, which I ran under the tap, then wrung almost dry. First things first. I had to get rid of the dust, or I'd be sneezing all day like Snow White's vertically challenged pal, Sneezy.

Once I had taken care of housekeeping and run back down the stairs to the store to pick up a carton of cream for my coffee, I poured myself a cup and sat down with the stack of mail in front of me. Mimi lay contentedly at my feet, having been indulged with a very large dog biscuit that I'd bought at the supermarket along with the cream and a raspberry Danish. She had calmed down somewhat over the past year, but could still raise hell when the occasion warranted—something like her mistress!

I'm Samantha Hope, though no one save those poor souls who toil away thanklessly as members of official government bureaucracy gets away with calling me that. I answer to just plain Sam. I'm single—well, divorced if the truth be known—and not much inclined to do anything to alter my marital state. Gabby and I, and our two Old English sheepdogs, get along just fine without the complication of adding males to the mix.

We live in a converted turn-of-the-century house in James Bay, an eclectic neighborhood in the heart of Victoria. The city, which boasts of being the warmest spot in Canada, is British Columbia's capital. Situated on Vancouver Island, off the West Coast, Victoria is isolated from the rest of the province by an hour-and-a-half ferry ride and, being the seat of the provincial government, from reality by the depth of the ocean that surrounds it.

Victoria is small as cities go and picturesque, relying on the tourist trade, the improvident spending habits of government, and old money for its economic base.

I had come to Victoria in the eighties, found work with a company that conducted consumer research, and hung in for ten years give or take, until last year when Bill came up with the bright idea of opening his own private investigation firm. Knowing that I was an incurable snoop and too curious by half, he sought to legitimize my questionable talents by offering me a partnership in his new company. I jumped at the chance.

After working on a couple of cases that turned into near-disasters, I decided, with more than a little pressure from friends and family, to take a hiatus from the business and concentrate on my writing. I write mystery novels, when moved by inspiration or the need to come up with extra cash.

Now, Bill was away, for God knew how long, and Gabby, my closest friend, recently announced that she had accepted a temporary teaching assignment in France. Her family was originally from Brittany, via Quebec, so she viewed the offer of temporary employment as a perfect opportunity to live in the old country while conducting family history research.

Gabby believes in reincarnation and has this crazy idea that she lived in Paris during the French Revolution. She is itching to see the Seine, Notre

Dame, and Montmartre, to find out if it's true. How she's going to manage that, I have no idea.

You can imagine that the idea of being abandoned, first by Bill and Emily, and soon to be by Gabby, was a bit hard to take. And Mimi wasn't going to be pleased either when she found out that Clem, Gabby's sheepdog and Mimi's constant companion, was going along with her to France.

"Just the two of us, eh Mimi?" I stroked her head and scratched her ears, and she preened, moving her head up and down to take full advantage of my caresses. "We'll manage. We'll find some trouble to get into, okay?" I asked. I took her silence as agreement.

That was my brilliant idea. On my way to the office, it had dawned on me that with my two main killjoys out of the way, there would be no one to stop me from taking on a couple of small investigations on my own. For Bill's sake, mind you. Hey, I wasn't planning on doing it just for my own satisfaction and enjoyment. Bill and I had put considerable time and effort into establishing the business, and I didn't want it to be all for naught. I would look after things—mind the store, so to speak—but just until he returned. And neither Bill nor Gabby would even need know what I was up to. After all, I *was* the HOPE of HOPE & HENRY. I had just as much right as Bill to play Perry Mason. I attacked the pile of envelopes I'd thrown onto the desk. Perhaps there would be something in the stack that I could sink my teeth into.

The mail was a big disappointment. Nothing but bills, a few pieces of junk mail, and a couple of checks from past clients for services rendered. Bill had left me a checkbook full of signed checks, just in case. I wrote out several and addressed the envelopes for them, to pay the bills. Then I locked up the office and, on my way home, stopped at the Credit Union to deposit the incoming checks in Bill's account.

Gabby opened the door before I could. "Guess what?" Her eyes sparkled with excitement.

"I can't imagine. Please don't keep me in suspense," I said grumpily. Faced with her imminent departure and my subsequent total boredom, I had been feeling sorry for myself for a few days. Even the prospect of running amok at the office hadn't succeeded in cheering me up.

"I've got a chance to leave for France earlier than originally planned. The school called. One of their instructors cancelled out for the summer session. They've asked me to fill in for him. They want me there at the beginning of July."

My heart sank. I didn't have the strength to tell her what a downer her news was. I had thought she would be around for the summer at least. I had been looking forward to camping trips and long walks at French Beach with her and the dogs. I wasn't great company all by myself. And July was only a week away.

"Great! I'm happy for you, Gab," I said somewhat insincerely. Then I tried to overcome my own misery and show support. "This is something you've wanted to do for a long time, so I'm glad you'll finally have the opportunity."

"Hey Sam, why don't you come over to France for a visit this summer? You love France."

That much was true: I *did* love France, at least what I'd seen of it. I'd never been to Brittany, but Paris and the South were fabulous. What I liked most of all was the French habit of sitting around drinking endless cups of coffee and munching on croissants or French baguettes for hours on end. However, my lack of work over the past year had resulted in my dipping into my savings big time. In a word, I was broke. I didn't think I could swing it.

"I'll think about it," I said, implying by my tone that I had all kinds of exciting plans of my own and didn't know if I could fit it into my busy schedule.

"Well, I'd better get busy," Gabby said. "All of a sudden I have only a short time to get packed and ready to leave. Lucky for me, I've already got my passport. I'd better call about flights though, and I have to arrange passage for Clem too."

"Are you really sure you want to take her along?"

I asked, hoping the answer would be no. I should have known better. Gabby and her dog were not easily parted.

"Absolutely. I couldn't live without her for a whole year. And besides, the French love dogs. She'll be my ticket into all kinds of places that I might not get to see otherwise. She might even help me meet a dashing Frenchman," she joked, laughing at my startled look.

"If you *have* to go to the trouble of finding a man, and why would you want to, wouldn't it be better to find one here? What if you fall madly in love over there and decide not to come back?" I grumbled.

"Don't worry. No man, no matter how exciting, could keep me away from home for long. I'll be back, you can bet on it."

"That's reassuring. Now what can I do to help?"

Chapter Two

The week flew by and before I knew it, I was driving home from the airport, Mimi at my side, having taken Gabby to catch her flight. Clem had departed the day before, to be picked up by Gabby at the Charles de Gaulle airport upon her arrival. I was feeling abandoned by everyone I loved. First Bill and Emily, now Gabby and Clem. Who next?

For the rest of the afternoon, Mimi made matters worse by searching the apartment high and low for Clem, and running to the front door every time she heard a sound. She was almost as pitiful as I was.

Jill Stone, our next-door neighbor, called and invited me for dinner, but I didn't have the stomach for it. It would have meant putting up with her husband George's superior attitude, which was annoy-

11

ing at the best of times and intolerable at the worst. I wanted to stay home and sulk, which I did very well.

That night Mimi, who normally slept outside my bedroom, was allowed inside. She stretched out at the foot of the four-poster bed and kept a close watch over me all night. Perhaps she was afraid I too would disappear and she'd be left alone. I understood just how she felt.

I had a difficult time finding a good reason to get up the next morning, but after giving myself a stern lecture, I decided that I couldn't mope indefinitely so I'd better get my act together and get on with my life, such as it was. Besides, Mimi was clamoring to go out for a run. I let her out and took a shower while she investigated all her favorite smells in the back garden. By the time I came downstairs to put on the coffee, she was waiting at the back door to be let back in.

"So, what are we going to do to keep busy today, Mimi?" I asked.

She studied me, her head cocked to one side, then came over and laid it on my knee. The next thing I knew, she was standing at the closet near the front entrance where her leash was kept, barking and scratching at the door.

"Oh, all right. Just let me finish my coffee and I'll take you for a walk."

I should not have said the *W* word until I had my coat and sneakers on. Mimi doesn't understand *wait*, or *just a minute*. When she heard the word *walk*, she began to run up and down the hallway, barking furiously.

"All right already! I'm coming." I gulped the last few mouthfuls of my coffee, swallowing a bunch of grounds in the process, and put my cup into the sink. "Let's go," I said.

I opened the door, and Mimi was outside and down the stairs in a flash. I had to call her back and make her sit so I could fasten her leash. We started up St. Vincent Street, crossing over Government Street and heading for the park.

Beacon Hill Park is our favorite haunt. One of our regular walks takes us straight through the park and across Dallas Road to the ocean. There is a path several miles long that twists and winds its way along the shore, ending at a grassy area where dogs and their owners congregate. Mimi is much more social than I am. She loves to hang out in this spot with her canine friends.

On this particular day she strained at the lead as we walked through the park, not bothering to stop and investigate every bush and bug as she usually did, but leading me straight to Dallas Road.

We waited at the crosswalk for the traffic to stop, then ran across the street into the field. Once on the other side I unbuckled her leash, and she took off like a bullet, running around in circles, then heading straight for an unsuspecting dog owner whose back happened to be turned toward us. He was totally unaware that ninety pounds of dog was headed straight for him.

I hollered at the top of my lungs to warn him of the impending collision but, with a stiff sea breeze blowing my words right back at me, I may as well have saved my breath. Mimi, oblivious to anything but her own pleasure at being in her favorite spot, ran straight into the man, hitting him squarely in the back of his knees and causing his legs to buckle. Did I mention that Mimi desperately needed a trim? Her vision was totally obscured by the long hair that hung like a curtain in front of her eyes. Clumsy at the best of times, she was even more so when she couldn't see one foot in front of the other.

The guy went down with a thud and a loud series of expletives. Mimi looked surprised, but she got up and gave herself a shake. Pleased to have brought this human down to her level, she planted a huge paw on either side of his face and began to lick. Judging by his attempts at evasive action, the man was not impressed, though once he realized she was friendly and not planning to chew his ears, he gave up and let her go to it. His own dog, a small cocker spaniel, and only a puppy at that, came bounding over to investigate. She managed to get Mimi's attention, and the two of them took off chasing circles around each other and barking happily.

By this time I had reached the man, who was still sitting on the ground. "Can I help you up?" I offered politely, trying to make up for Mimi's bad manners, though it was all I could do to keep from laughing. He and Mimi had created quite a spectacle.

"No thanks, I can manage." The man got up and brushed himself off, before turning so I could see his face.

"You!" I said as I recognized him. It was Fraser. What the heck was his last name? McDermott, that was it. I had met him about a year before, when I was working on the Gillespie case. He was an undercover cop and he and Trevor, who had been teamed with Bill years ago, before he retired, had been working on a drug case that had become intertwined with our investigation into Allison's disappearance. We had ended up collaborating, after a fashion.

Fraser. Who would have guessed! At the time we'd met, I *had* found him kind of sexy. In fact, I had thought that he and I just might hit it off, become an item.

I recall having had a good laugh when he had introduced himself as Fraser. At the time, he had been dressed in black leather and his head had been completely shaved. The name had seemed incongruous with his get-up. He was dressed much more conservatively now, but still sported a close haircut that showed off his nicely shaped head. His tan looked as though he'd gotten a jump on summer by vacationing down South. When we were working on the Gillespie case, I'd dropped a hint or two that I might be *at home* to him if he called, but he hadn't picked up on it. A year had passed with no contact. Darn Mimi anyway. She'd just ruined any chance I might have had to make a good impression.

"Sam, isn't it?" Fraser asked, a gleam in his eye. Or was it just the reflection of the bright summer sunlight bouncing off the nearby water?

"None other. Sorry about that." I pointed at Mimi. "She can be such a klutz."

"I seem to recall Trevor saying the same thing about you," he said mildly. "He warned me to stay a mile away from you or I'd get hurt. I guess he wasn't joking." His sexy smile took the sting out of his words.

I couldn't help but laugh. What was the point of getting mad? What he said was true—there was no denying it.

"Nice to bump into you anyway," I said, grinning back. I wasn't going to let him get the best of me.

"Hmm . . . for you perhaps." He looked down at his jeans, which were covered in mud. "I guess I'll have to cut my walk short and go home and change."

"Too bad—I was going to suggest we meander

over to Starbucks on Cook Street and I'd buy you a coffee and one of their decadent cookies by way of apology."

I thought I saw a momentary look of regret steal across his face. For a second, it appeared as though he might change his mind and say yes, or suggest an alternate time and place, but the moment passed and he merely said, "Sorry, I can't today. Perhaps some other time." The tone of his voice suggested it might be another year or longer before I saw him again.

"Okay," I said nonchalantly, though my pride was wounded. "Another time then. Come on Mimi, let's go," I called out to Mimi, who tried to ignore me at first, then came reluctantly to my side.

I turned and walked away. Mimi followed. She kept stopping and looking back at her newfound friend. I was too stubborn to do likewise.

For the rest of the day, Mimi and I were at loose ends. Jill called again, and this time, since she happened to mention that George was working late that night, I accepted her offer of dinner. She, more than anyone, knew how close Gabby and I were, and how difficult it would be for me with her gone. Besides, I was a lousy cook. I left Mimi at home and went next door.

When I got back some time later, there was a message on the answering machine. As I listened, Gabby's voice came through loud and clear.

Sam, bonjour! *Just wanted to let you know I arrived safely. I'll have my computer set up in the next couple of days, so check for messages, okay? I picked Clem up when I arrived in Paris. She's fine. I don't think she liked flying though. She sure was glad to see me. The rental car I arranged was waiting for me at the airport. In fact, everything's been great. So far so good.*

I listened morosely, annoyed at having missed her call. At the sound of her voice, Mimi's ears perked up, and she barked. But even she seemed to sense the distance between Gabby and us. She slunk to her mat as soon as the machine clicked off. In spite of my own misery, I was glad to hear that her trip had gone according to plan. In a day or two, she and I would be able to talk back and forth on the computer. She had set mine up and shown me how to use the e-mail and instant messenger before leaving.

Just as I was getting ready for bed, the phone rang. I thought it might be Gabby calling back, though I should have known better. Always a good money manager, she would not waste a dime on a second call, particularly as she had already left a message when she couldn't reach me the first time.

"Hello?"

"Sam, Fraser here."

Be still, my beating heart. I certainly hadn't thought *he* would be calling, especially as he had been rather abrupt at the park.

"Long time no see," I said tritely.

He laughed.

That's good, Sam. He seems to like your jokes. It's a start. "I hope you've recovered from your little mishap?" I asked.

"It was nothing a little soap and water couldn't take care of. And how are you?" he asked.

"Oh, just ducky. My three best friends in the world have gone away and left me alone, but other than that, everything's wonderful," I whined, wondering all the while why I was confiding my woes to a relative stranger.

"So you're all alone?"

"Just me and my dog. Why?"

"Well, I was wondering. . . ." There was a long pause.

"Yeah?" I asked.

I wasn't going to make it easy for him. There's *nothing* easy about me. I'm stubborn, opinionated, and difficult to get along with. He might as well know that, right from the beginning. *Beginning of what, Sam?* I asked myself. *I don't know,* I answered.

"What I mean is, how about you and I getting together some time?"

"I thought this morning would have been nice," I said, delivering a mild rebuke.

"Sorry, I was on the job. You know how it is."

"Oh." I should have known. After all, men are not totally immune to my charms. And I had thought I'd detected more than a slight interest in Fraser's demeanor when we first met.

"So how about it?" he persisted.

I'd have to give him credit for tenacity. "Okay. When?" I replied.

"How about now?"

"It's a little late." I glanced at my watch. Actually it was only nine o'clock; it just seemed later since I had put in a very boring day, which had made the time pass more slowly.

"Okay," he conceded. "How about tomorrow? Can we meet for coffee?"

"Why don't you come by the office around eleven?" I suggested. I had every intention of going into Bill's (and my) office every couple of days, just to keep on top of things—and in the vain hope that something would come up that I could get involved in to pass the time. I gave him the address, and we hung up.

I went straight to bed, not giving myself time to have second thoughts about meeting Fraser the next day. Sooner or later, one had to plunge back into the cesspool of dating and relationships. Surrounded by my friends and family, I had been satisfied to ignore that side of my life since the breakup of my marriage a few years previous. But I wasn't cut out for celibacy over the long haul. Fraser had been the first man in a very long time to pique my interest. Even at that, it had taken a year for things to foment before we advanced to the stage of a coffee date. At this rate it would be years before I had to make any really hard decisions—like whether I would subject him to my cooking. Or let him read my books.

So why did I set my alarm to get up a whole hour earlier than usual the next morning, so I could pluck my eyebrows and shave my legs, and why did I haul out the iron and run it over my jeans and T-shirt? I have no idea!

Chapter Three

I arrived at the office at about ten the next morning, having left Mimi at home. The extra hour gave me time to make a pot of coffee, listen to the couple of messages on the machine, and take a look at the mail that had arrived the day before. There were only a couple of envelopes. One contained a begging letter. The other looked more interesting. The address on the envelope had been hand-written, and there was no return name. I slit it open and removed the single, folded sheet of paper.

The letter was addressed to Bill, but I didn't let that stop me from reading it. But when I glanced at the signature my heart stood still for an instant, then pounded erratically to make up for the skipped beat.

It was signed *Walter Robins*. My father! What the heck was *he* doing writing to Bill?

The letter started out by admonishing Bill not to tell me that he'd written, as he didn't want to upset me. It went on to say that he had run into a spot of trouble and thought that given Bill's profession he might be able to help. He said he didn't want to reveal too much in the letter, in case it fell into the wrong hands. He asked Bill to call him and suggested that on his next visit to Victoria, perhaps they could meet without my knowing. What in heaven's name could be bothering my father so much that he didn't want me to know about it?

It had only been a couple of years since I had finally tracked him down, having grown up thinking that my mother's second husband, Hugh Hope, was my father. Once I learned that he was, in fact, my stepfather, I had gone in search of my birth father, finding him in Vancouver. He was happily remarried, to a woman named May Robins. His name was actually Richard Howell, but he had taken May's surname and called himself Walter, his middle name, to guard his privacy. When he and my mother had divorced, he had gotten into trouble—too much booze and the wrong kind of friends—and had ended up doing a stretch in jail. He had told me he used May's last name to avoid being harassed by some of the less than reputable pals he had acquired in his old life. He didn't want the past cropping up to cause difficulties for May—or for the rest of us, for that matter. Once I'd had a happy reunion with my father, I had arranged for him to meet with my older sister, Martha, and her family. Richard loved his grandson, Timmy, and, I'm sure, would do anything to keep him safe.

I read the letter over and over, trying to figure out what to do about it. Bill was gone, and wouldn't be back for several months. If my father had written to him, it meant that whatever problem he was facing must be serious, otherwise he would have handled it himself. He needed help now, not in a few months.

The worst of it was that I couldn't say a thing to him about his letter or his request for help. I would have to pretend I knew nothing. That would be hard, if not impossible. I knew myself well enough to know that I would have to find a way to help, with or without his knowledge.

"Sam, am I too early?"

Startled at hearing a voice, I looked up and saw Fraser standing in the doorway of the office. I hadn't heard him climbing the stairs and without my early warning system, Mimi, his arrival was a complete surprise. Seeing the letter had made me forget why I had come to the office in the first place. Quickly, I pulled a file folder over Richard's letter to hide it, and stood up.

"Fraser, hi . . . no, you're right on time," I said, looking at my watch. "It's right on eleven."

"Good. I hate being late." He advanced into the office and looked around.

"So this is where you and Bill hang out. Love the name on the door." He smiled. "*Hope & Henry*. How did you convince Bill to give you top billing?"

"I didn't. I just went ahead and got the sign painted and, since I was paying, he couldn't complain. Anyway, it sounds better than *Henry & Hope*, don't you think?" I gave him my sauciest look.

He laughed. "So, are we going out for coffee?" He looked over to the corner where the full pot of coffee was sitting on the counter.

"What?" I said, still feeling completely distracted by my father's letter.

"Coffee. Can I pour myself a cup, or are we going out?"

"Oh sure, help yourself." I waved my hand in the direction of the pot.

"Hey Sam, am I disturbing you? You seem a little out of sorts this morning. Would you prefer to be left alone?" he asked.

"No, of course not." I hesitated. Could I trust him? I decided to take a chance. "Sit down. Do you mind if I pick your brain?"

"It's a little early in the day. I don't know what you'll find in there," he joked. "But you can give it a try. What's up?"

I handed him the letter and waited silently while he read it through. When he had finished he looked up with a puzzled expression on his face. "I don't understand."

I filled him in on my relationship with Richard, a.k.a. Walter Robins, and told him my father's story—at least as much of it as I knew—and about how we had been reunited only a short time before. I told him how Richard had been an alcoholic, gotten into trouble, and gone to jail, and later, when he got out, joined Alcoholics Anonymous and turned his life around.

"He's not a young man anymore and his health isn't that good," I concluded. "I need to find out what the problem is and get him some help. But Bill isn't going to be back for a while. And from the sound of it, this can't wait."

"I see what you mean. And *your* hands are tied. You don't want him to find out you've read his letter. What do you have in mind?"

"I don't know. I just found the letter a few minutes before you arrived. I haven't had time to come up with a plan. What do *you* think?" I didn't give him time to answer. "What I need is to find someone who can pretend to be Bill and set up a meeting with my father. Richard has never actually met Bill; he just knows about him and the business from me. And he thinks I'm no longer involved, since last summer. Which I haven't been, up to now," I explained.

"Do you have anyone in particular in mind?" Fraser asked, a peculiar look on his face.

"No. I'm at a complete loss. Not just any man will do. It would have to be someone who's capable of actually helping, once he gains my father's confidence."

As I puzzled over this, Fraser got up and paced the room.

"Sam, what if *I* contacted your father? I don't want to impersonate Bill, but what if I told him that Bill had left me in charge of the business while he's away? I could arrange to meet him. After I heard his story, you and I could figure out how to help, depending on what the problem is. If it requires any legwork, you could do whatever is needed while I'm working, and I could help you when I'm off-duty. Your father wouldn't have to know you're involved."

"You would do this?"

I turned my face away because I didn't want Fraser to know just how much his offer had touched me. I mean, we hardly knew each other. He had absolutely no reason in the world to get involved in my problems, never mind my father's. But here he was volunteering to help out, even before he knew what he was getting into. What a guy!

"Sure. It can't be too serious. If it were, he would have gone to the police, wouldn't he?"

"I doubt it," I said. "He has a real distrust of authority, stemming, I suppose, from his time in prison. He could be in real trouble. I don't think he would have taken the drastic step of contacting Bill unless something was seriously wrong."

"Why don't we find out? Let's call him."

"Now?" My heart skipped a couple of beats. I was afraid to call Richard and find out what was the matter.

"Have you got his number handy?" Fraser persisted.

"I know it by heart. I'll dial, then I'll sit and listen while you talk to him." I picked up the phone, then hesitated slightly. "Are you sure about this, Fraser?" I wanted to give him one last chance to bow out. Being a cop, he saw enough trouble through his work without becoming embroiled in other people's problems in his off-duty time.

"Make the call. It's going to be all right, Sam," he said, trying his best to reassure me.

I dialed my father's number, and when the phone started ringing I handed it to Fraser.

"Hello, Mr. Robins?"

Fraser introduced himself and explained that he was filling in for Bill while he was away on his honeymoon. He asked if there was something that he could do to help. Richard said he didn't want to discuss the problem on the phone and suggested he come to Victoria to meet with Fraser. They set up a time for Richard to come over, the following week. After arranging the time and place for the meeting, Fraser said good-bye and hung up.

"There, now that wasn't so hard, was it?"

Little did he know. I would have liked nothing better than to be able to take care of the problem myself. "I hate having to admit that I need anyone's help, let alone a virtual stranger's," I said, then stopped short as I realized that, with typical Sam tact and diplomacy, I was being terribly rude.

Fraser laughed out loud at the look on my face. "Don't worry, I know just what you mean. And I agree we don't know each other very well. I suggest we try and remedy that before I meet your father. Now, what about that coffee?"

"Is it too early for a drink? I feel as though I need a good stiff one," I said.

"I know just the place. It's almost noon. We'll call it lunch. Let's go."

Chapter Four

Fraser and I had a long, lazy lunch. At the end of it he escorted me home in a cab. I hadn't forgotten about my father and his problem, but the blow had been softened a little, in part by a good meal, but mostly because I had confidence in Fraser's ability to help. Between us we would sort out the situation, whatever it was.

Fraser had set up the meeting with Richard for Friday afternoon. They had agreed to meet at three o'clock at the Empress Hotel, where my father would be staying.

I wracked my brain trying to figure out how I could observe the meeting between Fraser and Richard without being recognized by either of them.

Above all else, I knew I must not let Richard know that I had read his letter to Bill. For one thing, he had asked Bill not to tell me, and for the other, I didn't want him to know I was involved in the *snoop-for-hire* business again. He might blow my cover with Gabby, when they spoke to each other. There wasn't much danger of them bumping into one another with Gabby in France, but she might call for some reason—probably just to see how he and May were doing—and he might let something slip.

Fraser had promised me that after he met with Richard, he'd come to my apartment and report what had transpired. From where I was sitting, that was just not good enough. I mulled over my predicament until the day before the rendezvous. Then that evening, as I was walking along the causeway at Victoria's inner harbor where street musicians were performing for tourists, I saw a clown. It struck me that if I could come up with a good disguise, I could go to the Empress, sit near Richard and Fraser, and eavesdrop on their conversation without being recognized. Why not? I convinced myself that it was a brilliant idea and, since I was the only person I had to convince, I set about putting my plan into place.

I went right out and bought a grey wig. Then I hit the local thrift shops and bought an old-fashioned, flowered dress, a big, floppy hat, and a pair of sturdy black shoes. I had often observed that to a large percentage of the population, women over a certain age were, for all intents and purposes, pretty much invisible. Certainly to those of the opposite sex, in any case. I had no idea at exactly what age this phenomenon happened, but as I myself was rapidly approaching forty, I was curious and rather apprehensive. Nevertheless, the information served me well in coming up with my disguise.

I practiced walking with a cane. There had been one kicking around the apartment since the time Gabby had broken her ankle skiing.

Over the course of the next day, I tried on my costume several times, making slight alterations until I was satisfied with the look. At the last minute I traded the brown cane for a white one, and added a pair of oversized dark glasses. No one would be worried about me seeing them, if they thought I couldn't see at all.

Thursday night Richard called. I had wondered if he would arrange to see me while in Victoria for his meeting with Fraser; however, he merely chatted for a couple of minutes, asked how everyone was, and hung up without saying anything about his impending visit.

Friday afternoon, I got all dolled up in my fancy duds. *I* thought I looked great. When it was close to three, I walked the couple of blocks to the Empress Hotel, which was situated across the street from the inner harbor. One of Victoria's oldest hotels, the Empress was the veritable heart of the city, with her beautiful rose gardens and ivy-covered brick and stone.

I forced myself to walk slowly, using my cane to guide me. Once, when I stopped at a crosswalk, a couple of young people offered to help me across the street. I accepted, pleased that they were convinced I needed assistance.

I waited until just after three before going inside the hotel. As was the custom, tea was being served in the lobby.

Fraser was already seated at a table in the corner. He was alone. And I was in luck—there was an empty table next to his. A few people were in line ahead of me, waiting to be seated by the headwaiter. One of them was my father. He had his back to me. I prayed he wouldn't turn around. I didn't think he would recognize me, but you never know.

The waiter soon led Richard to Fraser's table, and Fraser stood up to greet him. The two men shook hands and sat down. Richard's back was turned toward the table I had designated as mine. I just hoped the waiter wouldn't seat anyone else there in the interim.

Luckily, the people waiting in line in front of me were all together and there were too many for the small table. The waiter led them to the opposite side of the large room. Finally it was my turn.

"Table for one, madam?" he asked.

"Yes please."

"Right this way."

The waiter turned to the right, as if planning to lead me to a table near the window. That was no good; it was too far away from Fraser and my father.

"The light bothers my eyes, young man. May I have that table in the corner?" I asked, putting a quaver in my voice and pointing to the table I wanted. The waiter looked at me strangely, as if wondering how I knew where I wanted to go when I couldn't see. Nevertheless, he led me silently over to the table I had pointed out. My nerves were jumping with the fear that I might be discovered.

I sat in the chair directly behind Richard, even though the waiter politely pulled out the one opposite. He came around the table and pushed in my chair, shrugging his shoulders as if to say, *silly old biddy*. Handing me a menu, he went back to attend to the growing line of patrons waiting to be seated.

I had seen Fraser glance at me, then away as I approached the table. *God, I hope he didn't recognize me,* I thought. Actually, I must say I felt pretty confident, smug even, that my disguise was good enough to fool him and anyone else, including my father. How could he know that it was me, hidden under all those ruffles, flowers, and hair? Besides, the hat and dark glasses prevented him from getting a good look at my face.

My ears cocked, like Mimi's when she thinks she hears the word *cookie*, I listened to the conversation between Fraser and Richard. They had ordered coffee and pastries, and while they were waiting for the waiter to bring them, they got acquainted. Richard gave Fraser a sketchy account of his history, including explaining his relationship to me. After their coffee arrived and the waiter left them alone, Fraser led the conversation around to the problem that had brought Richard over to Victoria.

"You said in your letter that you needed help. What can I do?"

"First, by way of explanation, I need to give you a bit more background. I've told you how Sam's mother and I were divorced. Well, I got in with the wrong crowd and ended up involved in a robbery. I got caught and went to prison. While inside, I was bunked in with a guy named Bob Patterson. He had done a lot of time. The most recent stretch was for robbing a bank. He used to brag all the time about the robbery. One night he let it slip that the money he'd stolen had never been found. He had managed to stash it somewhere before being arrested. He said that when he got out, he was going to go and find the money and take off for Mexico. I gathered there was a lot of it. Money, I mean. The problem is that one night when he was shooting off his big mouth, he actually told me where the money was hidden. Believe me, I would have preferred not to know," Richard said bitterly.

"I got out of prison before he did. I met May, we got married, and I decided to use her last name so that I could avoid situations like this. Didn't want him or anyone else finding and bothering me. I wanted a clean break with the past.

"The other day I got a call from Patterson. Somehow he had tracked me down. He said that when he got out of jail, he'd gone to collect his money from its hiding place, but someone else had gotten there first. He says I'm the only person who knew where the money was. He thinks I took it, and he's threatening to hurt me and those I love if I don't give it to him."

"Do you have any idea where the money is?" Fraser asked.

I waited anxiously for my father's response.

"No, of course not. Patterson was the kind of guy who never stopped talking; he bragged about everything. He was a big blabbermouth. He probably told a whole bunch of people where he'd hidden the money. Myself, I never really believed it existed, to tell you the truth. I thought he was just trying to look big.

"The problem is that Patterson has a mean streak a mile wide. I saw him take on a few guys inside, and no one ever got the better of him. I don't trust him not to make good on his threat. I don't care about myself, but I won't let him do anything to hurt my family."

Richard pounded his fist on the table, making their coffee cups jump and the spoons rattle in their saucers. Two elderly tourists at the next table watched him nervously. I imagined Fraser putting his hand on Richard's arm to calm him down.

"Hold on a minute. Do you know where Patterson is?"

"He didn't say. He's called a couple of times, but all he told me was that if I didn't give him his money back, he'd come looking for me. He gave me a deadline. It's almost up."

I could hardly contain myself. It was all I could do not to jump up and tell Richard not to worry, that Fraser and I would help him somehow. But I knew I had to keep my big mouth shut and trust Fraser to take care of the situation.

"Tell me all about Patterson. He must have told you something about himself. Does he have a family? Where's he from? Do you remember anything that could help us figure out where he might be? We need to find him before he comes looking for you."

"I don't know much," Richard replied. "I know he grew up in Vancouver. And I know he wasn't the only person involved in the robbery. A couple of his buddies were in on it. He used to gloat about how they didn't know where he'd hidden the money either. He told me that, at the time of the robbery, they didn't get caught. He was real proud that he never squealed on them either. He alone paid the price for doing the job; that's why he figured he didn't have to share the spoils," Richard concluded.

"If you don't know where we can find him, we may have to wait until he calls again and try to set up a meeting. How do you feel about involving the police?"

"No way!" Richard was adamant. "If any of my old pals got wind of it, I'd be a dead man. I have to handle this without involving the cops."

Lucky he didn't know he was talking to a cop. Perhaps once Fraser had his confidence, he would be able to convince him that going to the police was the best course of action under the circumstances.

"Okay, if you feel that strongly about it, I won't insist. Here's what you do. Go home. Wait for Patterson's call. When it comes, agree to meet him. Then call me right away. Try to arrange it so I can make it over to Vancouver in time. You know the ferry schedule from the Island to the mainland. Just make sure you allow enough time for me to get there. I don't want you meeting him on your own. Do you understand?"

"Sure. Actually, I'm not looking forward to meeting him, alone or with someone else. He's a nasty character, a real louse. And prison didn't straighten him out; he just got more and more bitter as time went on. Of course he was convinced the system had done him wrong."

"Now, don't forget to call me as soon as you hear from him. I'll give you a couple of numbers where you can reach me."

Fraser must have given Richard a piece of paper. Their chairs scraped against the marble floor as they stood up. Richard left. My eyes followed him to the exit. I gathered up my purse and reached for the cane.

"Sam, what the hell were you thinking?"

Darn! *Stay calm, Sam,* I said to myself. *Dressing up in funny-looking clothes and a wig is not a criminal offense.*

"What? Oh hi, Fraser."

Fraser had stayed behind when Richard left, and now he was closing in on me with an angry look on his face.

"How was coffee?" I asked lamely, chagrined at having been caught in my little subterfuge.

"Never mind coffee. Let's get the heck out of here. You look ridiculous."

He grabbed my arm and pulled me to my feet. I picked up my white cane and walked, ever so slowly, to the exit. Onlookers watched me as if they thought I was an escapee from an old folks home, or a kleptomaniac caught in the act of making off with the silver.

"Cut the theatrics," Fraser said, giving me a push from behind to speed our departure.

"Darn it all, let go of me," I said, shaking myself free. "You didn't expect me to just sit at home and wait for your call, did you?"

"That's *exactly* what I expected."

Fraser's lips were tightly closed over his nice white teeth. No smile for me. His hand on my back was sending all kinds of pleasant sensations rushing through me; however, I didn't think the timing right to explore them further, so I shuffled a little faster to the hotel door and down the front stairs to the sidewalk.

"I'm taking you home," he said, signaling for a cab.

I was whisked away unceremoniously. Once inside the cab, I took off the dark glasses and smiled sweetly at Fraser, who scowled as he gave the cabby my address.

"So what about that story? My father's, I mean?" I asked.

"Not another word until we're home," he said, warning me sternly.

"Yes, sir!" I saluted facetiously. I absolutely hated anyone giving me orders and usually did my best to ignore them.

The rest of the short ride passed in silence. When we arrived in front of the house, Fraser paid the driver and came around to the other side of the cab to open my door. I got out awkwardly, knocking my outrageous hat askance in the process.

"Let's get inside before any of the neighbors see you." He looked around to see if anyone was watching, but the street was deserted.

"Don't you worry about *my* neighbors. They'll be firmly on my side, I can assure you. They're quite used to me," I said.

I made for the front door, pulling out my key and unlocking it. Mimi, who had apparently been waiting just behind the door, took one look at me and started barking.

"Oh for heaven's sake, Mimi, it's only me," I said, yanking off the wig and kicking the horribly uncomfortable shoes, which felt as if they were a full size too small, halfway across the room.

"So what are we going to do to help my father?" I asked Fraser, who by this time had begun to see the humor in the situation and had collapsed on the sofa in the living room, laughing uncontrollably. His laughter got Mimi barking and, for a moment, bedlam ensued.

He reached up and grabbed me, pulling me down onto his lap. "You are one crazy woman," he said, as his lips came down on mine.

Chapter Five

"Seriously, Fraser, what are we going to do? I'm really worried about Richard."

I had gone and changed out of the flowered dress into a pair of jeans and an oversized shirt. I'd washed the makeup off my face and rinsed my hair, drying and combing it into something resembling my usual style. The grey wig was lying in the corner, Mimi guarding it as though it was an errant sheep. Things were slowly returning to normal.

"You have every right to be worried," Fraser replied. "It's not a good situation. The first thing I'm going to do is try and find out something about this Patterson character. It won't be hard to get more info on the robbery, or on his sentence. Perhaps he's on parole. If so, I may be able to find out where he's living. I'll use the time while waiting for your father's call to try and track Patterson down. The only problem is, I'm going back on duty for four days starting tomorrow so I won't have much time." His face revealed his concern.

"What can *I* do?" I asked. I wasn't prepared to sit around for the next four days waiting for Fraser to get off duty again.

"That's a little more tricky. Remember, your father doesn't want you to know what's going on."

"You're right. But I can't just sit back and wait for something horrible to happen," I complained. Waiting was not my forte under any circumstance, never mind when family was involved.

"Let's see what I find out," Fraser said. "I'll call you as soon as I know anything more. In the meantime, you could call Richard every day or two just to check on him, or better still, why not make a quick trip to Vancouver? Find an excuse to go for a visit."

"Hey, that's a great idea! I can tell him I'm working on a story and need to do some research in Vancouver. What do you think?"

"That might work. But promise me you won't go looking for Patterson. That would be downright stupid," Fraser said, a warning in his voice.

"I promise," I said, crossing my fingers behind my back. Everyone knows if your fingers are crossed, promises don't count.

* * *

The next evening, having given him time to get back home, I called Richard and told him my story about needing to do some research for a book I was writing. In actual fact, I had been going through a dry spell and hadn't written anything since my mystery on the Gillespie case had been published.

"It's not really convenient for you to come over right now," Richard said, perhaps reluctant to have me visit in case he heard from Patterson again.

"I promise I won't get in the way," I said, using the old guilt weapon to make it hard for him to give me an outright no.

"Never you mind him," a voice called out in the background. May must have snatched the phone from Richard, as she came on the line and insisted that I come over whenever I wanted. Evidently Richard hadn't told her about the call from Patterson. She seemed puzzled at his reluctance to see me. Since it hadn't been that long that he and I had re-established our long-dormant father–daughter relationship, he usually jumped at the opportunity for a visit.

"Right-o. You'll see me on Monday after lunch then."

Richard came back on the line. "It's not that I don't want to see you, Sam," he said. He stopped short of explaining any further.

"I know, Dad." I didn't explain how I knew what he meant either.

That evening, I finally got around to sitting down to the computer, which I had been avoiding, since it irked me to sit at my desk and not be able to write. However, I wanted to check my e-mail to see if Gabby had written me from France. I turned on the computer and started the software program that connected me to the Internet and to my e-mail.

A little icon showed that a letter was waiting in my mailbox. I clicked on the icon and a list of mail popped up on the screen. Actually there were two messages, both from Gabby.

Sam, formidable! *This place is so great! I love Brittany. It's so clean. The houses are all whitewashed and the roofs are made of dark tiles. They look like gingerbread houses with icing. I'm settling in nicely and so is Clem. I'm staying in a little cottage on the edge of campus. I understand it used to be the gardener's cottage in the days when the chateau was occupied. Did I mention that my landlord lives in a converted chateau? It's right here on campus too. There's lots of room for you to come and visit this summer if you decide to. I'll be starting to teach the computer course on Monday. Clem and I miss you and Mimi. I sure hope you figured out how to get into the e-mail; you didn't forget your password, did you? I guess not, if you're reading this. I'll write again on Monday after class. Hope everything is okay at home.*

Love, Gabby

The second message said,

Sam, I forgot to tell you that I have a chance to go to Paris next weekend. My landlord, Jean-Claude, is driving into the city on Friday and he offered to take me along. If I can arrange for a hotel room, I'll probably take him up on his offer. I'll finally get a chance to see the Seine.

Bye for now, Gabby

I clicked on the reply button and sent the following message.

Dear Gabby, everything's just peachy keen here. Mimi and I are having a ball. I went for tea at the Empress the other day. Too many grey-haired grannies for my taste though! And you remember Fraser, the cop we met last year; the one who hangs around with Trevor? Mimi and I ran into him the other day. Glad things are going well, and that Brittany is so clean. Jean-Claude? Give me a break! Why is he going to Paris anyway? It's probably just a ruse to get you alone! I'll check for mail again on Monday.

Cheers, Sam

I found it inexplicably depressing to communicate with Gabby by electronic mail. She seemed so close and yet so distant. I decided not to tell her about Richard, or about Fraser and me trying to help him. It would only worry her.

I took Mimi with me to Vancouver on Monday, along with my laptop so that I could keep in touch with Gabby. Richard and May wouldn't mind about Mimi, and without Gabby at home, I couldn't leave her behind. She had never stayed in a kennel, but I already knew that she wouldn't appreciate it. She was too spoiled by half.

We arrived at Richard and May's place just after lunch. I hugged them both, even though it's not my favorite thing to do, relieved that they had not come to any harm since Richard and I had spoken on Saturday.

"Sam, it's good to see you," May said. As we hugged, she whispered in my ear, "I need to talk to you. I'm worried about your father."

"Sure," I replied. "Just give me a minute to chat with him, and I'll meet you in the kitchen."

"What are you two plotting?" Richard said, coming up behind May and putting his arm around her.

"Nothing that concerns you," May answered cheekily. "I'll go and put the coffee on. Have you had lunch, Sam?"

"I ate on the ferry, if you can call that eating. But I could go for a cup of coffee. And do you have any cookies?" I teased. May always baked when she knew I was coming for a visit.

"So, tell me what you're writing, Sam," Richard said. "Another mystery?"

"Yes, and I'm branching out," I replied, lying through my teeth. "I have decided to set the story in Vancouver. That's why I needed to check out a few spots. I like to use real place names and locations for color. I'm nothing if not accurate."

"I see you've got Mimi with you." Richard had glanced out the window and seen her sitting in the driver's seat of the van. "You'd better bring her in."

"I will, and I'll get my overnight bag too. I hope it's not too inconvenient to have us here."

"No, no. You know you're always welcome, Sam."

May called from the kitchen. "Sam, can you come and help me with the coffee tray?"

"As long as you don't want me to cook anything, I should be able to handle it," I called back to her and headed for the kitchen.

"What's up?" I asked.

"It's your father. He's been acting really strangely. He won't let me answer the telephone. Every time it rings he makes a mad dash for it. One of these times he's going to fall and break his neck. And he keeps going and checking the doors and windows, to make sure they're locked. It's like living in a fortress around here."

"Has he said anything at all?"

"No, I asked him if anything was wrong, and he said there was nothing. But something's up, I know it is. Maybe you can get him to tell you what's bugging him."

"I'll try," I said, wanting to reassure her. I knew very well what was wrong, but was hesitant to say anything to May. I wasn't sure how she would react or whether she'd be able to keep from saying something to Richard. I didn't want him to know that I knew.

"How's that coffee coming along? With the two of you working on it, shouldn't it be ready by now?" Richard called out to us.

"Hold your horses," May retorted. "Here, take this tray in to your father. See if you can get him talking." She handed me the tray, and I carried it into the living room.

Several times I did my best to steer the conversation around to a place where Richard would be able to talk about the situation with Patterson, but he wouldn't bite, deflecting me each time.

When I finished my coffee I brought Mimi in from the van. She made the rounds, soliciting attention from everyone before settling herself on the carpet in front of the fireplace.

I told Richard I wanted to take a short drive, to begin looking for a good location for a murder. His face paled.

"Dad, I'm just joking. I'm talking about my story."

"Oh yes, your story," he said, looking relieved. "You *will* leave Mimi here with us while you go out, won't you?"

"I'm sure she'd love that. But don't feed her too many cookies. She's such a mooch."

As if she understood, Mimi got up and went over to Richard, laying her head on his knee. He patted her soft fur and slipped her one of May's freshly baked cookies.

"You see what I mean?" I asked. "Who can resist her? She's so sweet."

"She's a good watchdog too, isn't she?"

"Let's just say she's noisy. She'll bark like crazy if she hears anything, but don't count on her after that. She's very friendly, as you know."

"Barking's good. Good girl, Mimi," Richard said.

I got up to leave. "I'll be back in time for dinner."

"What? Oh, sure, Sam. See you later."

Chapter Six

What was I going to do to keep myself occupied for the rest of the afternoon? I had no idea. I hopped in the van and backed out of the driveway, no particular destination in mind.

As I started up the street, I spotted a dark blue late model Ford sitting across the street from the house. Its engine was running. The man in the driver's seat turned his head away from me as I passed, so I didn't get a good look at him. I proceeded to the corner, all the while wondering if the guy was Patterson. Why would someone be sitting in a car in front of the house with his motor running? With the high cost of gasoline these days, who could afford to? I speculated that it might be Patterson; he could have Richard's house staked out. Was he merely watching the comings and go-ings, or did he have something more sinister in mind? Or was the guy in the Ford just an innocent man—an oxymoron if I've ever heard one—waiting for a friend to come out of a house across the street?

At the corner I turned right and pulled over just far enough down the street to be out of sight of the Ford. Something told me to hang around until the vehicle either took off or the guy got out of it and afforded me a better look. I climbed out of the van and walked back toward the corner. Hiding behind a big, old oak tree on the boulevard, I waited to see what would happen next.

I didn't have to wait long. Without warning, the car pulled away from the curb and started toward the corner. I sucked in my stomach and tried to make myself invisible behind the tree trunk. My heart pounded furiously. The Ford stopped at the stop sign, turned left and sped away.

In a split second I made a decision, one of those deserving of a lot more study and consideration than I gave it. I jumped back in the van, did a U-turn, and raced after the Ford. By the time I got turned around, the guy was a couple of blocks away, but there was no one else behind him so I was able to keep him in sight. I moderated my speed slightly so I wouldn't catch up to him, then followed at a more sedate pace.

While I was driving, I fished in my purse for a

pen and piece of paper. With one eye on the Ford and the other on the paper, I wrote down the car's licence number. Fraser would be able to run it through the system and find out who it belonged to.

The driver made a series of turns, and I followed. Then, for no apparent reason, he pulled over and stopped. The only thing I could do was to continue driving past the parked car and to try to appear uninterested. As I came alongside the Ford, I chanced a look at the man behind the wheel. He was big and burly with curly dark hair. His nose leaned slightly to one side as though it had been broken at some time in the past. The sleeves on his shirt were rolled up to the elbow, and he had a tattoo on his left forearm. I couldn't make out what it was.

Could he be Patterson? I wished Richard had told *me* about Patterson, so I could ask what he looked like. I cast back in my mind to Richard's conversation with Fraser at the Empress Hotel, but I couldn't recall Richard having given Fraser a physical description of his former cellmate.

I happened to have my cell phone in my purse so, once I was far enough away from the Ford not to look suspicious, I pulled over to use it. I had Fraser's pager number. I didn't know what hours he was working, but thought to use the pager first before trying him at home. It dawned on me that I had neglected to tell him that I was coming to the mainland, however, it had been his idea in the first place, so he wouldn't be surprised.

When the answering service picked up my call to the pager, I left my name and number. Then I sat back to wait for a return call. The Ford hadn't moved. I could just barely make it out in my rear-view mirror. I sat tight to see if the driver would get out of the car or continue on his way. There was no movement for a good half-hour and no return call from Fraser either.

Finally the Ford pulled away from the curb. This time it drove past me, and the driver glanced in my direction. I got another look at his face, which was mean and menacing. Did he realize I had been following him? Probably. I wasn't too good at being circumspect; blatant was more my style.

I waited until a couple of vehicles had formed a line behind the Ford before pulling out again. Following at a safe distance, I dogged the Ford for a couple of miles, until we reached the Kingsway area of Burnaby, the neighboring community to New Westminster. May and Richard actually lived in New West near the Burnaby border.

Finally the Ford turned off Kingsway, making a right into the parking lot of an older-style apartment building. *Mr. Mean and Nasty* got out of the car and locked the door. He used his keys to open the outside door of the building and disappeared inside. I was tempted to take a look at the list of residents next to the intercom but having been caught doing this once before, I was leery. I could always come back, now that I knew where he lived. If, in fact, he did turn out to be Patterson.

The cell phone jangled and made me jump so high I bumped my head on the interior roof of the van.

"Hello?"

"Sam, where the heck are you? I've been trying to call you at home. All I get is that ridiculous message on your answering machine. Trust me, you'll never get work as a comedian."

Fraser sounded exasperated. I don't know why, but I seem to have that effect on people at times.

"And here I thought I was funny." I had composed my message using a British accent and pretending to be Queen Victoria. Evidently Fraser was not amused.

"Think again. Anyway, you didn't answer my question."

"Actually at the moment I'm in the van, in Burnaby, sitting in front of a dilapidated apartment building, having followed a car here from in front of my father's house in New West. Could you check out a licence plate for me?"

"What the . . . ! I thought I told you not to try anything funny," Fraser sputtered at the other end of the line.

"Funny, who's funny?" I quipped. Then more

seriously, I said, "Hey, you said why didn't I go to Vancouver to visit my father? That way I would be able to keep an eye on him. I came over this morning. I told Richard and May that I'm doing research for a new book. We had coffee. I said I was going out to check on some potential sites for a murder. For the book, I mean. When I went outside, I saw a guy sitting in a car across the street. He seemed to be watching the house. So, when he pulled away from the curb, I followed him. He led me to Burnaby, just off Kingsway, to this apartment building. He parked and went inside. I think he lives here. He had a key to the front door. I'm still sitting in front of the building, waiting to see if he comes out again. Now, can you check on the licence number of the car for me or not?"

"Sam . . ." His voice went up a couple of decibels. "I told you I didn't want you doing anything dangerous, without me there to help."

"And I told you I wanted to help my father," I replied. So there! I'm afraid I let my impatience be heard in my voice.

"Give me the damned number. I'll check it out and call you back."

"Thank you," I said.

"What are you going to do now?"

"I'm going to do what I told Richard I was doing. I'm going to drive around and look for a good location for a future book. Then I'm going to go back to the house for dinner. Does my itinerary meet with your approval?"

"Don't get your back up, Sam. We're supposed to be working on this together, remember?"

"How can I forget? Why is it that whenever men get involved in anything, they try to take it over? Can you tell me that?"

"Just tell *me* something. Who's the cop?"

I didn't have a smart answer for that question, so I replied with a question of my own.

"When are you getting off work?"

"I have to work tomorrow, but I'll be finished in time to get the last ferry over to the mainland. I've got a friend in Burnaby that I can stay with. I'll call you from his place when I arrive."

"But you'll call back on the license before then, right?" I didn't want him holding out on me.

"Right. Quit being so paranoid," he said.

"Okay, I'll wait for your call." I hung up. Men!

That night during dinner my cell phone rang again. I excused myself and went into the kitchen to answer it. It was Fraser.

"Sam, you've got to promise me that you won't do anything stupid until I get there tomorrow night."

"Me? Stupid? Surely you jest?"

"Sam," he insisted, a threat in his voice.

"Okay, okay."

"I checked out that licence number you gave me,

and it's you-know-who. Look, I did a quick background check on him too, and he's one mean dude.
Believe me, you don't want to tangle with him. He
wouldn't have any qualms about messing up that
pretty little face of yours if he gets wind of the fact
that you've been watching him."

"Why thank you, Fraser, I didn't know you
thought I was pretty."

"SAM, are you listening to me at all? This guy is
not to be messed with." He sounded ready to jump
right through the phone.

"Yes, I heard you. And don't yell at me."

"Sam, is everything okay?" Richard had come
into the kitchen and caught the tail end of the conversation. Had he heard me mention Fraser's name,
I wondered.

"Everything's fine, Dad. I'll be right there."

"What?" Fraser asked, and I said that I had been
talking to my father.

"Sam, promise me you'll wait until I get there
tomorrow night before trying to check out Patterson
any more."

"Fraser, I have to go," I whispered into the phone.
"Call me when you get over."

I hung up without promising anything. Since I
had already decided I was going to go back to the
apartment, I didn't want to have to break my word
yet again. Now that I knew it had been Patterson
who was parked outside the house, I wouldn't be

able to stay away. I would turn the tables on him and see if I could find out what he was up to. I put the phone in my purse and went back into the dining room.

"Now, where was I?" I asked, as I sat down to my dinner, which had congealed on the plate in my absence.

"Give me your plate, Sam, and I'll zap your dinner in the microwave," May offered. I handed her the plate.

"Are you sure everything's okay?" Richard asked.

I studied his face to see if there was any sign that he had overheard my conversation with Fraser, but saw only concern.

"Fine. It was just a friend. He's planning to come over to the mainland tomorrow night and wants us to get together for a drink."

"Anyone we should be meeting?" Richard was always telling me to find someone nice and settle down *just like Martha.*

"Not yet. But who knows? Anything can happen. If anything does develop, I'll be sure and let you know." I winked, then laughed as he smiled back at me. That was the first smile he'd given me since my arrival.

"I'll be waiting to offer my sincere condolences to the man who gets tangled up with you, Sam. He'll have his hands full!" Richard's eyes twinkled.

"Dad!" I protested.

He was right, though. I was no bargain. It would have to be a special man with lots of courage, to take me on. I didn't know if Fraser was the one. He seemed to be an extraordinary human being, no doubt. But how would he react when he realized that I was a free spirit, and not at all appreciative of anyone who tried to tell me what to do, or to control my behavior, even with the best of intentions?

After dinner, I excused myself and set the computer up in my bedroom, so that I could write a note to Gabby. After resolving the minor glitch of having to find an access phone number for Vancouver, as opposed to the one I used in Victoria, I ran my mail program. Yes, there it was, a reply to my message of a couple of days ago.

Sam, c'est magnifique! *You know, I just love this country. People are so friendly here. Sure, they smile at my accent when I speak French, but then, when they learn I'm Canadian, they call me* cousine. *They think I'm from Quebec. They've never heard of Victoria. Imagine that! Jean-Claude found me a room at the hotel where he'll be staying in Paris; he'll be just down the hall. He offered to take me out sightseeing when we get there, but I said no thanks.*

I want to see the Seine by myself. You know, in case I do something silly, like bawling my eyes out. I told him we could perhaps have dinner one evening. Give Mimi a dog biscuit and a hug from me. One of my students has volunteered to look after Clem while I go to Paris. Clem has already made friends with the lot of them. I hope you're managing to stay out of trouble?

Love, Gabby

I pressed the reply button. What to tell her? That was my dilemma. There was no point in getting her worried about Richard's problem or about my involvement in it when she was too far away to help. Yet, I couldn't keep her completely in the dark. Sooner or later she was bound to try and get me on the phone, and she'd find out I wasn't at home.

Hey, Gabby, sounds like you're having a super time. Mimi sends her love—to you and to Clem. I'm writing to you from the busy metropolis of Vancouver. I decided to come over for a bit of a visit with Richard and May. I'm going to make Vancouver the setting for my next book.

There! Keep your story consistent, Sam. That's a good strategy.

I ran all over town today, looking for a good site for a mystery—even staked out a couple of locations and watched the people coming and going. You know, there's a lot that goes on in the city that most people are not aware of. It's a real education. Now about Jean-Claude. He sounds like a sly one. At the very least, demand a room one floor above or below his. Don't make it too easy for him. Hope you enjoy the Seine. I highly recommend taking a ride on one of the bateaux-mouches *that cruise up and down it. Do it at night so you can see the lights of* Gay Paree. *But my advice is to leave Jean-Claude at home.*

Love, Sam

Chapter Seven

The next morning the sun came out. Since it had been a rare occurrence of late, I volunteered to do a little yard work for Richard and May. I cut the lawn and weeded a couple of the flowerbeds in front of the house. After lunch I told Richard I wanted to do some more scouting in the neighborhood and, after taking a shower and changing into clean clothes, I took off in the van, leaving Mimi behind once again, admonishing her to look after Richard and May.

I'm sure I don't have to tell you where I headed. As soon as I left my father's, I drove straight to the apartment building on Salisbury Street, pulling up across from it. I checked out the parking lot, but couldn't see the Ford. Patterson appeared to be out.

I decided to chance it and sneak a look at the list of tenants on the wall next to the door. Patterson's name wasn't there.

As I was standing in front of the door, wondering what to do next, an elderly woman opened it and came out, smiling at me encouragingly.

"Can I help you?"

"I was j-j-just looking for a friend," I stuttered, chagrined at having been caught off-guard. At least it wasn't Patterson. "I think I have the wrong place."

"What's your friend's name? I know everyone in the building," she said proudly.

"Louise Petersen. Do you know her?" I asked, giving her the first name I could think of.

"Petersen? No, there's no Petersen. Now, there *is* a Patterson. Bob Patterson. He lives with Mary Lucas on the third floor. Apartment 303. There's no one named Louise in the building. Sorry I can't help you." The woman gave me another smile and set off down the sidewalk with her purse and a mesh shopping bag over her arm.

Actually she had been a *big* help. I checked the tenant list and found Mary Lucas's name. The lady was right; Lucas's name was opposite apartment number 303. Walking quickly back to the van, I pulled a notebook from my bag and wrote down the name and apartment number before I forgot it.

What to do next? I sat for a moment, pondering the information and trying to decide on my next move. What I should have done was to get the heck out of the neighborhood, but I must confess I was a little too complacent for my own good. I didn't even notice Patterson's Ford approaching from behind, nor did I hear it stop and the driver get out. The next thing I knew, his big, ugly face was pushed up against the car window, peering in at me. Not only was it peering but the face was attached to a body, and that same body had a hand attached that held a gun pointed at my head.

"What the hell are you doing here?" Patterson yanked open the door of the van and jabbed me in the shoulder with his gun.

"Nothing, nothing at all," I stammered, my heart pounding. My knees went weak, as adrenaline pumped through me at an alarming rate.

"Get out."

"Will you put that gun away, please? You're making me nervous," I said, smiling weakly.

"Now ain't that just too bad." *Mr. Mean and Nasty*'s face contorted in a grin. "Shut up and get out of the van."

He jabbed me again with the barrel of the gun, and I didn't dare refuse. I slid off the seat and out of the van. My feet hit the ground and I grabbed hold of the door jamb for support.

"Now, you and I are going for a little walk," Patterson said. "I'm going to put this gun in my pocket and walk behind you. Don't get any bright ideas. Just act normal."

Normal! My friends could have told him that he was asking the impossible. "Where are we going?" I asked.

"Never mind. Just cross the street and walk slowly to the door of the apartment. Remember I'm only one step behind you, close enough to blow your brains out. Don't try anything stupid."

Now stupid, that was more my style! I could do stupid with both hands tied behind my back. I forced myself to stay calm, and did as he ordered. Just as we arrived at the other side of the street, I noticed the same little old lady I'd seen a few minutes earlier, walking back down the sidewalk toward the apartment. We arrived in front of the building at exactly the same time.

Totally ignorant of what was taking place right under her nose, she came up to me, smiling broadly.

"Did you find your friend?" She glanced over at *Mr. M & N* and back at me. "I see you found Mr. Patterson. Silly me, I forgot my umbrella. Last night that nice young weatherman on the television news said there was a risk of thunderstorms today. I don't want to get caught in a shower without my umbrella."

I grabbed my chance. Somehow I didn't think even Patterson was mean enough to interfere with a nice little old lady, especially one who knew his name. I took her arm.

"Here, let me help you. What did you say your name was?"

"I don't think I did, young lady," she tittered. "It's Mrs. Jackson."

"Mrs. Jackson, I wonder if I might trouble you to let me use your telephone? I might be able to find my friend if I can take a look at the phone book. I must have written down her address incorrectly. You don't mind if I come up to your apartment with you, do you?" Please, pretty please!

"Of course not. Come on upstairs." She turned back to *M & N* and said, "Nice to see you again, Mr. Patterson. Say hello to Mary for me."

He growled a reply, turned abruptly, and walked away without a backward glance. Mrs. Jackson opened the door with the key. I almost tripped over myself, and her, in my haste to get inside the apartment building and out of Patterson's direct line of fire. Once inside I collapsed against the wall, watching as *M & N* got into the Ford and drove away. I was sure I hadn't seen the last of him, but at least I had a reprieve.

"You know, I have to confess, I'm not too fond of Mr. Patterson," Mrs. Jackson whispered at me from behind her hand. "They say he just got out of prison. Mary told everyone he had been away working on an oil rig off the East Coast, but I think she was fibbing. He's not very friendly at all. Most of the people in the building are very nice, but I find him quite surly. I do so like a man with nice manners, don't you, dear?" She studied me earnestly.

"Yes, I do, Mrs. Jackson, I certainly do," I agreed. "You know, I think I'm just going to go home now. I'll visit my friend another day." I wanted to get the hell out of the neighborhood before Patterson returned.

"Are you sure?" she asked. I nodded. "Well, all right, I hope you find your friend. I'm going to go upstairs and get my umbrella. Then I must go back out and do my grocery shopping."

"Thanks so much for your help," I said.

She said, "You're welcome," though she had *no* idea just how much help she'd been.

I didn't waste any time getting into the van and driving away. That was too close for comfort. I vowed to be more careful next time, if, God forbid, there *was* a next time.

I didn't want to go directly to Richard's, in case *M & N* was waiting somewhere around the corner to pounce on me again, so I drove around aimlessly for over an hour, checking the rear-view mirror every few seconds to make sure I wasn't being followed. Of course he knew where Richard lived, but still I didn't want to take him home with me and tip off Richard to my run-in with him. Once I was sure that I was alone I headed home. I would lay low until Fraser showed up that night.

Back at the house, Richard met me at the door with a grim look on his face.

"Sam! I've been worried sick. We have to talk," he greeted me.

"What's the matter," I asked, puzzled that he was so upset.

"I had a phone call a few minutes ago. Come and sit down."

I followed him into the living room. "Where's May?" I asked. I had noticed the car was gone, when I drove into the driveway.

"She went to the store for groceries and to run a few errands. I want to talk to you before she gets back."

"What's the matter, Dad? You seem worried."

"I am, and with good reason. Sam, I know you know all about Patterson."

How had he found out?

"He called here a few minutes ago. He told me to ask you about your little encounter with him. What was he talking about?" Richard paced up and down the room as he spoke.

"Dad, sit down." How had Patterson known who I was? "Yes, I do know about Patterson. Fraser, the fellow you met in Victoria? He's a friend of mine." I didn't tell him that Fraser was also a cop, just in case he refused further help from him, once he knew. "When your letter to Bill came to the office, he was away on his honeymoon. He had asked me to check on the mail so I happened to be there. I opened it, not knowing it was from you. When I read that you needed help, I asked Fraser to talk to you, since you seemed to want to keep me in the dark about whatever was happening." I tried to keep the reproach out of my tone, but he picked up on it.

"I was only trying to protect you," he interjected. "I didn't want to involve you or the rest of the family."

"I know, and I appreciate it, but I want to help. I was sitting behind you at the Empress Hotel when you met Fraser. He and I agreed that I should come over to New Westminster, so I could keep an eye on you and May. Fraser does shift-work, so he wasn't able to get away. But he's coming over tonight, and we can sit down with him and try to come up with a plan."

"Whatever possessed you to follow Patterson? He said on the phone that he had seen you following him yesterday, and today you were sitting outside his apartment building when he came home. He said that you and he had a little conversation."

Thank God Patterson hadn't told Richard about the gun! "That's right. I saw him sitting in front of your house yesterday. At that point I didn't know who he was, although I had my suspicions. I followed him to his apartment. I got Fraser to check out the licence plate number and verify that it *was* Patterson. Today I went back to the apartment to make sure that he actually lived there. I found out he lives with a woman named Mary Lucas. Did he ever talk about her when you were in prison?"

"No, I don't think so." He hesitated. "No, wait a minute, I seem to recall, about the time I was released, he mentioned he had started writing to someone named Mary. A lot of women write to men in prison. Sometimes one thing leads to another. Why are women so fascinated with characters like him, I wonder? Yes, I do remember him saying something. But never mind that. What happened today?"

"He confronted me in front of the building. Just warned me off. Nothing serious," I said hastily when I saw his worried look. "Now at least we know where he lives. If he continues to threaten you, we'll call the police."

"No, I don't want to do that," he said quickly. "I'll handle this my own way," he insisted.

"Dad, be reasonable. This guy is dangerous. You need help."

"I know I need help. That's why I wrote to Bill. And Fraser has promised to help. He seems very capable. I want you to stay out of this, Sam." His look was one of determination. I recognized it because people tell me I have one just like it.

"I can no more do that than fly to the moon, so you may as well save your breath," I said. At least I knew where my stubbornness and pig-headedness originated. My father was as bad as I was, perhaps worse. "We're in this together and we're going to find a way of dealing with it together."

"If you insist," he said reluctantly. "But for Heaven's sake don't say anything to May about Patterson," he admonished. "I don't want to worry her."

"Don't you think, for her own safety, that she should know what's going on?" I asked, hoping he would agree.

"No, I don't," he replied quickly. "Why does this have to be happening, just when things were finally going so well for us? I'm happily remarried now and I've been reunited with you and Martha, after disappearing from your lives for so many years. Then there's little Timmy, my grandson. Everything has been just perfect. And now this. I guess what they say is true; your past *does* come back to haunt you," he complained bitterly.

"Dad, don't panic. Fraser will know how to handle the situation. He's great, and he'll be here later tonight. In the meantime we have to stay calm. Why don't I make us a nice cup of tea?"

"It's times like these, I could really use a drink," he replied.

"That never solved any problems before, did it?" I quickly reminded him.

"Don't worry, I'm not really serious. I'd never go back to my old lifestyle. But there are times when I'm sorely tempted."

"We'll get through this, I promise."

Chapter Eight

We sat and drank several cups of tea while waiting for May to return from her shopping trip. When it got close to six o'clock and she still hadn't shown up, we began to get worried.

"Where do you suppose she is?" Richard asked, parting the living room curtains and looking nervously out the window. "She's usually not this late. Do you suppose she's had car trouble?"

"I don't know. Where does she shop? I could go and look for her," I offered.

"Would you, Sam? She always shops for groceries at the Safeway store on the corner of Eighth and McBride. It's not far from here. She said she only had a couple of errands to do. She was going to get the groceries last, so they wouldn't have to sit in the car too long. Then she said she'd be home to prepare dinner. Something's wrong, I know it."

I grabbed my purse and fished around inside it for my keys. "You stay here, in case she calls. I'll go to the Safeway and see if I can find her. Lock the door behind me and don't open it to anyone but May or me. I'll call as soon as I find her. I've got my cell phone with me." I held it up as I headed for the door.

The Safeway was only a few minutes away by car. I drove up and down the parking lot until I found Richard and May's car, heaving a sigh of relief at having spotted it. May must be inside the store. I pulled in next to it and went into the big grocery store, searching up and down the aisles to see if I could find her. There was no sign of her anywhere. I checked and double-checked every aisle to make sure I hadn't missed her. Then, with a deep feeling of foreboding, I went back outside.

I had parked next to the passenger side of May's car. Now, as I walked toward the van, I noticed that the driver's door of her vehicle was slightly ajar. How could I have missed that? Holding my breath and fearing the worst, I looked inside. The keys were in the ignition, and two bags of groceries were sitting on the back seat.

Patterson! He must have driven straight from harassing me to Richard's house, seen May leave and followed her to the store.

Quickly, I removed the key from the ignition and locked the car door, being careful not to touch anything in case there were fingerprints. Jumping back in the van, I made a beeline for home.

I didn't have to worry about the fingerprints. The kidnapper was self-confessed. Richard was standing on the sidewalk in front of the house as I drove up, and he already knew what had happened.

"Patterson's got May," he called to me as I stopped the van in the driveway and jumped out.

"Oh no, I was afraid of that. I found the car parked outside the Safeway with the keys still in it. Did he call you?"

"Yes, just a minute ago. He says he's not going to let her go until I give him the money. Sam, I don't have the money," he said imploringly. "And I don't have any way of coming up with it either. What am I going to do?" He stood ringing his hands and pacing back and forth, like a caged animal.

"How much money is involved?" I asked, thinking perhaps we could scramble around and come up with enough money to satisfy Patterson.

"He wants $250,000."

My heart sank. Neither of us had that kind of money, or any way of getting our hands on such a large sum. "Did he give you a deadline?"

"He said that he would call back tonight around midnight and tell me where to meet him."

His voice cracked and a tear squeezed from the corner of his eye and fell into one of the furrows on his face, coursing downward to his mouth. He wiped it away with the back of his hand. I steered him toward the front door and we went inside.

"Try not to worry. At least we know where he lives. We can talk to the police. Maybe they can break into his apartment and get her out, if that's where he's holding her."

"No!" he said urgently. "He said if we involved the police, he'd kill her."

"Well, what do you propose we do?" I asked, trying desperately to think of a solution.

"What if I suggest to him that he let her go in exchange for me?"

"How would that help? You're not thinking straight."

"Well, at least if he's going to harm someone, it shouldn't be an innocent bystander like May," Richard insisted.

"But you're just as much of an innocent bystander as she is. You didn't take the money, right?"

"You're right, I didn't. I only wish Patterson would believe me."

"He's a ruthless man. He wants his money and he doesn't care what he has to do to get it," I said, not thinking of the effect my words would have on my father.

"That's just what I'm worried about. I have to get May away from him," he said frantically.

"Fraser will be here later this evening. Maybe between the three of us we can come up with a plan. I'm going to try and get hold of him through his pager. Why don't you go and make us a sandwich? It will help us stay calm," I suggested.

"I don't know if I can eat anything," he said dubiously.

"Well, make one for me then," I said, looking for a way to distract him a little and keep him occupied. It's not going to help May if we get all upset. We've got to stay cool. I'm going to go into the bedroom and make a few calls, while you make the sandwiches. I'll come and help you in a couple of minutes."

I quickly went into the bedroom and shut the door. I dialed Fraser's pager number and left my name and number. I had made up my mind I was going to ask him to involve the police without Richard's knowledge or consent. At the very least, they could check out Mary Lucas's apartment and see if May was being held there. I suspected Patterson wouldn't be so stupid as to keep her there when we knew its location, but it was worth a try. And I would call Mrs. Jackson. She might have seen something. I figured she didn't miss much of the goings-on in the building. She might be able to provide some valuable information.

My cell phone rang, and I answered quickly.

"Sam, it's me," Fraser said. "What's up?"

"Lots. We've got a bit of a crisis on our hands." I explained quickly what had happened, first to me, and then to May. After he finished swearing at me, Fraser calmed down and agreed that it was a good idea to call in the local police detachment without mentioning anything to Richard. If nothing else, they could verify whether May was being held at the apartment, and perhaps talk to the building's residents and gather some helpful information.

"I'm stuck in the ferry line-up right now, but it looks as though I'll make the seven o'clock sailing. I'll be at your father's a little after nine. While I'm on the boat, I'll set the wheels in motion for a police search of the apartment. Don't do anything rash until I get there, please."

"I won't. I'll wait to hear from you. And thanks, Fraser. I don't know what I'd do without your help."

"Don't mention it."

He hung up, and I dialed Mrs. Jackson's number. There was no answer. I left a message on her machine, asking her to call when she got home. Then I went out to the kitchen to tell Richard that Fraser would be arriving in a couple of hours. In the meantime, we had to keep calm and wait for him and for the next call from Patterson.

As we were sitting at the kitchen table eating our sandwiches, it suddenly dawned on me that my father's telephone was an old-fashioned one that didn't have caller ID. In the event that Patterson was careless and called from a phone that wasn't blocked, caller ID might be a way of obtaining a phone number and, ultimately, an address for his hideout. After explaining this to Richard, I told him I was going to go to the nearest store to try and find one, and that I'd be back shortly. I ran to the van.

I didn't know my way around New Westminster all that well, but I did know the location of a late-night drugstore in Burnaby. It even had an electronics department that would be sure to have the kind of telephone I was looking for. The store also happened to be located just off Kingsway, not far from the Lucas apartment. I decided to head in that direction.

As I drove along Kingsway and arrived close to the turn-off for the apartment building, I couldn't resist the urge to take a slight detour and drive down Salisbury Street on the slim chance that I might see something that would help us find May. I couldn't bear the thought that *M & N* might do something horrible to her. She meant the world to my father. I had to do everything in my power to prevent that from happening.

* * *

Night was just beginning to fall and the lights were already on in several apartments. I didn't know the layout of the building so I had no idea which apartment was number 303, other than it was obviously located on the third floor. Somehow I came up with the bright idea of gaining access to the building by whatever means possible and checking the layout of the first floor. The third would likely be the same.

I thought about calling Mrs. Jackson again, and if she was home, asking her to let me in, but this proved unnecessary. As I approached the building, a young couple came out, holding the door open for me so I didn't need her help. So much for security, I thought, as I thanked them.

I stepped into the lobby and looked around. The decor was Spanish tacky, with bright red carpet on the floor, and red and gold wallpaper that had begun to curl around the edges on all the walls. Fake wrought-iron candleholders, strategically placed, held light bulbs that illuminated the hallways.

Two elevators faced the front door, and a corridor stretched in front of them from one side of the building to the other. A small sign indicated that apartments numbered 100 to 110 were on the right while those numbered 111 to 120 were on the left. I made my way down the right-hand corridor. The numbers ran consecutively, with number 103 being located almost in the middle off the hallway facing the street. As long as the third floor was identical, that gave me the location of the suite occupied by Mary Lucas.

I wanted to go back outside to see if there were any lights on in her apartment, but I needed to be able to get back inside the building, so I took a piece of paper from my purse and folded it into a small square. This I used to jam the latch on the door so that it didn't quite catch. I went outside to take a look.

Sure enough, lights were on in the Lucas apartment. Someone was home. Faced with this information, I wasn't sure what my next step should be. Glancing at the list of residents next to the intercom, I noticed that Mrs. Jackson lived in apartment 203, which, if my supposition about the layout was correct, should be right under 303. Impulsively I picked up the intercom and pressed the button next to Mrs. Jackson's name. The phone rang a couple of times, and she came on the line.

"Hello, Mrs. Jackson. This is Samantha Hope. We met this afternoon. I was the person looking for Louise—"

"Petersen," she interrupted, "yes, I remember." There was a pause, as she waited for me to explain what I was doing ringing her doorbell so late at night.

"Would you mind if I came up for a moment? I have another favor to ask of you."

By all rights, she should have said no; she didn't know me from Adam. But I was counting on curiosity getting the better of her. She reminded me a lot of my own neighbor, Mrs. Stevens, the biggest busybody around, yet a woman with the proverbial heart of gold. Unless I had totally misread Mrs. Jackson, she wouldn't be able to resist.

"Of course, Samantha," she replied. "Just a minute while I push the buzzer. I'm on the second floor."

Bingo! "Thanks so much; I'll be right up."

My heart in my throat, I rode the elevator to the second floor. I was worried that I might bump into Patterson, but both the elevator and the halls were deserted. I didn't see a soul, other than Mrs. Jackson, who was peeking out her door watching for me.

"Hello dear, come on in. I'll put the kettle on. Come into the living room and sit down," she invited as she bustled around, filling the kettle and putting it on the stove to boil. She seemed grateful for the company.

"Thank you so much for being so trusting. You know, you really shouldn't let strangers into your apartment," I admonished.

"If I didn't, you wouldn't be here, would you now?" she replied with a giggle.

"Now tell me what this is all about. You know, this afternoon I had a feeling that things weren't quite right. It's that horrible Mr. Patterson, isn't it? I told Mary that I thought she was very foolish to get involved with him. He's an unsavory character."

And I'm sure that Mary was just delighted to hear you say that, I thought. "You're right," I said. "This does concern him."

"I thought so!" She rubbed her hands in glee.

I gave her an abbreviated version of my father's story, and though she appeared shocked, she rose to the occasion like a Canadian version of Miss Marple, the famous Agatha Christie character.

"Okay, here's what I think we should do. I'll call Mary; she and I are quite good friends. I'll find out if Patterson is at home. If he isn't, I'll take you up there so you can meet her and get a look around. We can pump her for information while we're at it. What do you say?"

If I hadn't been so worried about May, I would have laughed out loud. All the world needed was another amateur detective! I quickly agreed. It was a golden opportunity for me to sneak a look at the Lucas apartment. If Patterson *was* holding May there, I'd find her. If not, at least I would be able to rule out this location and concentrate the search elsewhere. I sneaked a look at my watch. Eight o'clock. I'd better get a move on. "Okay, let's make the call. Do you have a second phone somewhere?"

She pointed to the bedroom. I waited while she dialed the number and, before Mary Lucas answered, picked up the extension. After three or four rings, Lucas came on the line.

"Mary, this is Helga. How are you?"

"Fine, Helga. About the same as when you saw me a short while ago," Lucas chided, giving me the impression that Helga made a perfect pest of herself where Mary was concerned. "How about you?"

"Fine. I have a friend visiting me this evening and I thought if you were alone, I would bring her up to meet you. Is Bob home?"

"No, he's gone out. He had some business to take care of. I was just going to get ready for bed though," Lucas protested.

"We'll only stay a minute," Mrs. Jackson said, dismissing her protestations. "I'd really like you to meet Samantha, and she's only in town for the evening."

"Okay, come on up," Lucas said, her resigned tone suggesting that she'd probably learned the hard way that there was no arguing with Helga Jackson.

"We'll be right there."

"Let's go," Mrs. Jackson said to me, as she turned the kettle off. "We'll have to have our tea later. And you had better call me Helga. We don't want Mary to suspect anything." Mrs. Jackson positively glowed with excitement.

"In that case, call me Sam," I replied.

Chapter Nine

W e took the elevator to the third floor and proceeded down the hall to Mary's apartment. She answered our knock right away.

"Mary, this is Sam. She's the daughter of an old
friend. I wanted you two to meet," Helga said, getting the introduction out of the way as she sailed
into the apartment like the Queen Mary into port.

Mary was a woman in her mid-fifties, with grey-
streaked brown hair and a face crisscrossed with
worry lines. She held out her hand, and I shook it
firmly.

"Pleased to meet you, Sam. Come on in. Helga,
should I put the kettle on?" she asked. "Do you have
time for tea?"

"We don't want to keep you from your bed,"

Helga protested insincerely, and settled herself on the sofa.

"Don't worry. I'll make a pot of tea then?"

"That would be lovely, thanks," I said. I looked around the small apartment trying to decide on an icebreaker. "You've done a wonderful job of decorating this place, Mary."

"Do you think so?" She beamed. "Just let me turn on the kettle and I'll show you the rest of it." She quickly filled the kettle and set it on the burner, turning it on high. "Right this way." She gestured toward a short hallway and a couple of closed doors.

I *oohed* and *aahed* over her frilly bedspread, and the handmade quilt that lay across the bottom of the bed. Then she showed me her study and the bathroom, in quick succession.

"Mary, the kettle's boiling. Do you want me to make the tea?" Helga called from the living room.

"I'll get it," Mary replied, giving me an apologetic look. "Excuse me for a moment, Sam."

"No problem." Actually I was delighted to have a couple of minutes to myself. It gave me an opportunity to check for a possible hiding place and for signs of May having been there. I went back into the bedroom and looked in the closet and powder room, then searched the study. The closet door in the study was hard to open. I tugged at it and it finally gave way. It had been blocked by a chair that was sitting just inside the closet door. Winter coats were strewn about the closet floor. I leaned inside and poked at them with my toe. My foot hit something hard that made a scraping sound against the linoleum.

I pushed the coats aside and hidden under the pile was a small black purse. I recognized it right away. *That's May's!* I thought. She and I had joked about the size of her purse because it was so small compared to mine, which held everything but the kitchen sink. I opened my bag, which was still slung over my shoulder, and dropped May's inside, my heart pounding in fear that I might be caught. So May *had* been here! But where was she now?

"What are those coats doing on the floor?"

Mary's voice startled me, and I jumped. She had returned from the kitchen.

"Honestly, men! Bob must have been looking for something in the closet. What a mess! And why has he got that chair in there? You'd think he'd have the decency to put it back where it belongs when he was finished with it." She picked up the chair and carried it back to the far corner of the room. "I'll pick up the coats later."

"Men, you can't live with them, can't live without them," I joked.

She smiled, a tiny wistful smile, as though she'd like to try.

Was she really as surprised at finding the chair in the closet as she had appeared? The rest of the apartment was spotless, obsessively so. It *did* seem out of character for her to have left the coats on the closet floor, if she knew about them.

I was betting that Patterson might have held May in the apartment temporarily while Mary was out, then moved her some time before she got home. Perhaps she worked during the day and had arrived home only a short while ago. I had to find out.

"Mary, what kind of work do you do?" I asked.

"I'm a social worker. I work with young people who are mentally disabled," she said proudly. "I went back to school when I was in my forties and began a new career."

"Good for you," I said. "Boy, that must be a very demanding job. Did you work today?"

"Yes, actually I just got home at around six. A crisis came up involving one of my clients. That's why I was planning to go to bed early. I get very tired. I'm not as young as I used to be," she admitted.

"You know, I think it might be better if we skipped the tea tonight. You probably have things to do before your husband gets home, and I should be going anyway. Perhaps some other time?"

"Bob isn't my husband," she confessed.

"How did you and Bob meet?" I asked, wondering just how far she would go in revealing her personal life to a total stranger. I have found that as a rule people are pleased when anyone shows an interest in their lives and will answer almost any question put to them. She did not disappoint me.

"Actually we met in prison," she said, looking embarrassed.

"Really? How did that happen?"

"It was just after I finished my social work degree. I was working in the prison as part of a practicum. After my practicum was finished, Bob and I kept in touch through letters and phone calls. When he was granted parole, he called me. One thing led to another, and here we are."

"And has it worked out as you imagined?" I asked.

"Not exactly," she replied, and promptly burst into tears. "I thought he wanted to go straight, start a new life." She didn't go into any detail about what had happened to make her change her mind. "That does happen, you know," she insisted, hiccuping noisily.

"I know. I could name someone in my own family who is living proof," I said gently. "Is everything all right, Mary? I realize you don't know me at all, but if there's anything I can do to help, I'd be happy to try."

"You're very kind, but I don't know if anyone can help."

"Why don't you try me?" I handed her a Kleenex out of my bag, and she blew her nose.

"Why Mary, what's the matter?" Helga had become impatient and came to investigate why we were taking so long. "You look as though you've been crying." She looked at me questioningly.

Trust Helga to interrupt, just when I was beginning to make some headway with Mary Lucas.

"Everything's fine, Helga. Sam says she has to go now though, so I guess we'll have to have our tea another time."

"Thanks for your hospitality, Mary," I said. I reached in my bag and pulled out one of my old business cards. "Here. If there's anything I can do, please call me."

She looked at the card and frowned. "Hope & Henry?"

"It's a company I used to be involved in. I'm not there any more, but the phone number is still valid," I explained, not wanting to scare her off. "I'll write my cell phone number on the back. You can reach me through it almost any time."

"Thanks." She tucked the card in her pocket.

"And now, I really must go. Helga, are you ready?"

"Yes. Good-bye, Mary."

Mary closed the door behind us, and right away Helga turned to me. "Did you find out anything?"

"Let's go back downstairs, and I'll show you."

Once we were back in Helga's apartment, she put the kettle back on. I glanced at the clock and asked if I could use the telephone. I dialed Richard's number.

"Sam, where are you? I've been worried sick. Is everything all right?"

"Fine, Dad. I got delayed. There was a huge traffic jam. I'm almost at the drugstore. I'll get the phone and be back there before Fraser arrives, okay?"

"Okay."

"Any more developments?"

"No, nothing."

"Be there soon. Bye."

I drank a quick cup of tea with Helga, telling her about finding May's purse in the closet.

"I'm going to give you my card too, Helga," I said when I got up to leave. "My cell number is on the back. If you see anything at all, please call me, no matter what time it is. I gave her a physical description of May, just in case Patterson brought her back to the apartment, though I didn't think he would. "And if you're talking to Mary, if she tells you anything that you think might help us find out where Patterson's hiding May, please let me know."

She agreed.

I hurried out to the van, started it, and drove up the street. As I neared the traffic light at the corner it changed to red, so I stopped and waited. Two vehicles came through the green light, turning off Kingsway onto Salisbury Street. Though neither had the typical red "cherry" on top, denoting a police vehicle, I spotted uniforms on the two guys in the first car. Coincidence? Or had Fraser made good on his promise to call the local precinct?

I continued on to the drugstore, made my purchase of a telephone with caller ID, and started back toward Richard's, retracing my earlier route so that I drove past Salisbury Street again. It was too dark to see if the unmarked cars were still in front of the apartment.

I arrived back at Richard's place just as Fraser was pulling into the driveway.

Chapter Ten

"Boy, am I ever glad to see you," I said to Fraser, as we met on the front porch.

"Any new developments?" he asked.

"Yes, but let's go inside and I'll tell both of you at the same time." I rang the doorbell and, without waiting, opened the door and walked in.

"Richard, are you there?" I called out to my father.

"Yes, in here."

His voice came from the living room. Fraser and I went inside. He was sitting in his easy chair, not comfortably as he normally did when he watched television or read the newspaper, but on the edge of his seat, his hand resting on the phone, which was sitting on the table beside the chair.

"Dad, you remember Fraser?" I asked gently.

My father had aged overnight, and my heart ached at seeing how vulnerable he looked, sitting there at the mercy of Patterson, who didn't give a hoot about him or May or the rest of us. All he wanted was his money, and he wouldn't let anything or anybody stop him from getting his hands on it.

"Mr. Robins," Fraser said as he advanced into the room, holding out his hand. "Don't get up."

"Sit down, Fraser. And please call me Richard. Sorry you've been dragged into the middle of this mess," he said apologetically.

"Never mind that. Have you heard anything more?"

"Did Sam tell you that Patterson called earlier and said he'd be calling again at midnight, to tell us where to take the money? I don't know how we're going to accede to his demands, since we don't have the money. Sam, did you get the telephone?" he asked, eyeing the plastic shopping bag I was carrying.

"Yes, Dad, why don't you go ahead and set it up? I thought it might help to have a phone with caller ID," I explained to Fraser.

I had to tell the two of them what I had found out. I fished into my handbag and pulled out May's purse. "Do you recognize this, Dad?" I asked, holding up the small black purse.

"That's May's. Where did you get it?" He jumped up out of his chair with more agility than I would have thought possible and grabbed the purse.

"It's a long story. Sit down and I'll tell you what happened."

I told Fraser and Richard everything, except about having seen the police arrive at the apartment as I left the area. That information I would tell Fraser as soon as we got a moment alone. I didn't want Richard to know the police were involved.

"So what next?" Richard asked. "I guess we still need to wait until we hear from Patterson." He looked glum. His hands played idly with the clasp on May's purse. He opened it and looked inside, then dumped everything out into his lap, carefully examining each article as though it might hold a clue as to where she could be found. He picked up a small metal notebook with a miniature pencil attached to it, opened it, and glanced inside.

"Look at this." His voice held excitement. "There's a note here. He held it out to Fraser, who got up and crossed the room to take it from him.

"*Find Blondie.*" He looked at Richard. "What do you think she means by that? Does May know about Patterson? About your connection to him and about him thinking you took his money from the bank robbery?"

"She didn't know before, but I'm sure he must

have said something to her when he grabbed her. I told you before what a big blabbermouth he is."

"And who's Blondie?" Fraser asked, turning to me. "Could that be Mary Lucas?"

"No, she has brown hair—well, actually it's a toss-up whether there's more brown or grey—but it's definitely not blond."

"You said Patterson was supposed to call around midnight, is that right?" Fraser asked Richard.

"That's what he said."

"That's just under three hours from now. What if you told Sam and me where Patterson said the money was hidden, and we went and checked out the area? How far away is it?"

"You'd never be able to see anything in the dark. It's a very wooded area." Richard looked desolate. "What are we going to do? We need to buy more time."

"What if we tell Patterson that you're going to try and come up with some money to replace what's missing, but you need more time. If we can get him to give us a day or two, we might be able to find out where he has May hidden," Fraser suggested.

"I hate the idea of May being in Patterson's company any longer than necessary, but what's the alternative? If we tell him we haven't got the money and can't come up with it, he's liable to kill her." He paused to give Fraser's suggestion some thought. Silence hung over the room like a thundercloud, casting a huge shadow and charging the air with electricity.

"I think you're right; we need more time," I said to Fraser. "Dad, we have to stall him. If we can make him believe that you have his money, or that you're going to do something desperate to get some so you can give it to him, he may agree to wait a little longer. I would really like to go to the spot where the money was hidden. There may be some clue, something we can follow up on, that will lead us either to May or to the money. And maybe we can discover who Blondie is and why May thinks we should find her. What do you say?"

"Sam's right," Fraser added. "We can't go looking tonight, since we wouldn't be able to find the spot in the dark. We need at least one more day. We know that May is okay, since she had the presence of mind to write the note and leave her purse behind in the apartment on the off-chance that someone would find it. If we can buy a little more time, we might be able to find her, or the money."

"I know you're both right. And if May was spunky enough to get a message to us, then we should try to follow up on it. What should I say to Patterson though? He's going to be suspicious, you know. He doesn't trust anybody, least of all me. After all, he thinks I stole his money."

"We've got a couple of hours. Let's try to come up with a plan," Fraser said. "But first, do you think you can make me something, Sam? I didn't get a chance to eat tonight when I got off work."

"If you're willing to risk it," I joked feebly. "Come and help me." I wanted to get him alone, so I could tell him about the police showing up at the apartment. Then he could call them and find out if they had learned anything that would lead us to May. "Dad, could you drink a cup of tea?" I called back to Richard as I went into the kitchen.

"Okay Sam, if you're making some," he replied distractedly.

He looked distracted as well. I figured he was probably cursing Patterson, and himself, for having gotten May into this situation.

"Don't worry, Dad. With Fraser helping us, we'll get May back."

"Sure," he said, though it was obvious he feared the worst.

In the kitchen, I told Fraser about seeing the police as I drove away from the apartment and he got right on his cell phone. He learned that when the police arrived at the apartment, no one was there. They had waited for some time to see if anyone would turn up. When an hour passed and no one showed, they had left to try and get a search warrant so they could enter the empty apartment.

Fraser explained to the police that I had been able to gain access to the apartment just before they arrived and that I'd found May's purse. Although she must have been there earlier, she had since been moved. He asked them to check into Patterson's background to see if they could find out from the investigation file if anyone had been identified as a possible accomplice to the robbery. He seemed to think that if we knew who else was involved with Patterson, we might get a line on who had stolen the money from its hiding place.

As I made Fraser a sandwich, we talked about what to do next. I suggested that if Patterson agreed to give Richard more time, we could get up early the next morning and go to the location where the money had been hidden. At the very least, the spot could serve as a jumping-off point for us, though by now, a few years later, the trail would likely be too cold to lead us anywhere, never mind to May.

As an alternative, I suggested contacting Mary Lucas again, explaining everything to her and trying to elicit her help. I didn't think she could possibly be involved in Patterson's scheme. But what would she be prepared to do to protect him? That was a big unanswered question. We would never know unless we asked. From my conversation with her earlier, it seemed that she had begun to doubt both him and her love for him.

It *was* strange, though, that she had not been at the apartment when the police arrived. Very little time had passed between my departure and their arrival, not enough for her to have gone very far. Did she know something was up, and was she shielding Patterson? Or was she simply out visiting a friend like Helga in one of the other apartments? I had thought she was planning to go straight to bed when we left her. Something must have happened to make her change her mind.

Fraser ate his sandwich, and Richard and I drank a cup of tea while we waited for Patterson to call. By midnight, we were all as jumpy as frogs in a pond. When the phone finally rang, it was almost anticlimactic. Richard picked it up on the second ring, while I sat next to him for moral support, my ear as close as I could get to the receiver so I could listen in. Fraser listened on the extension in the kitchen.

"Hello."

"Howell, I hope you've got some good news for me," Patterson growled belligerently.

"I want to talk to May," Richard said grimly.

"Don't worry, she's just fine, aren't you, May?" Patterson laughed into the phone, his voice grating like fingernails on a chalkboard.

The sound made my blood run cold. What a creepy guy!

"Let me talk to her," Richard insisted.

"Oh, all right." He must have handed the phone

to May as there was a long pause, then we heard her voice.

"Richard?" Her voice quavered as though she was on the verge of tears.

"May, are you okay? Has he hurt you? I swear I'll kill him if he harms you in any way."

"I'm okay. He hasn't hurt me. Just do what he asks please, so I can come home." There was a scuffling noise, and Patterson came back on the line.

"You see, Howell, she's just fine. Now where's my money? The sooner you give it back, the sooner you'll see your wife again."

"I need more time," Richard said. "I told you before I didn't take your money. I have to find a way to get my hands on some. $250,000 is more than I keep in my checking account. Give me a day or two. If I have to rob a bank myself, I'll get the money somehow. Just don't hurt May, or I swear I'll find you and kill you, I promise."

Richard had got up and was pacing around the room. His face got so red and angry that I thought he was going to have a stroke.

"Calm down, Richard," I whispered. "Stay calm, or you'll blow it."

He sat back down, and I listened with him again.

Patterson said, "I told you, just give me the money and no one gets hurt. I'll give you two days, then I'll call back. If you haven't got the money by then, you'll force me to do something drastic. I want my money, you hear," he screamed at Richard and slammed down the phone.

Richard was dripping with sweat and had the phone in a death grip, as though his hands were around Patterson's neck. I pried the receiver from his hand and hung it up.

I put my arm around his shoulders. "Okay, this is good news, Richard," I said, trying to calm him. May's okay, and we've got two days to track Patterson down and find out where he's got her hidden. It's going to be okay."

Fraser came back into the living room from the kitchen. "Did you check the caller ID?" he asked.

"I forgot all about it," I answered, grabbing the phone from its cradle. "It says *pay phone*. The number's here. Hey, I don't recognize the area code; that's not British Columbia. Where the heck has he taken her?" I grabbed my bag and searched for a pen and my notebook, writing down the number. "We need to find out where he was calling from."

"Call the operator. Ask what location uses that area code," Fraser suggested.

Richard, who, up to this point, had seemed oblivious to our conversation, got up from the sofa and came over. "Let me see that number."

I handed him the notebook, and he studied the telephone number intently.

"I know where this is. It's Washington State. Good heavens, he's taken her across the border;

we'll never find her!" He sank back onto the couch and put his head in his hands.

"Don't panic. There are ways of tracking down a phone number. We can narrow our search just by finding out the location of the pay phone. But we'll have to wait until morning. We can't do anything at this time of night. Now I know it's going to be hard to sleep, but I suggest you go to bed. I'm going to go to my friend's for the night, but I'll come back here tomorrow morning, bright and early. Let's say eight o'clock? And we'll get busy."

"You're right," I said. "Richard, why don't you go to bed. Even if you can't sleep, you can still get some rest. It's going to be a difficult couple of days. You need your rest. I'll let Fraser out and tidy up the kitchen. If you do manage to fall asleep, I'll wake you up at seven."

Richard got up heavily, shook Fraser's hand, and hugged me. As soon as he left the room, I turned to Fraser.

"Can you get us some information on the location of the pay phone?"

"Sure, piece of cake. As soon as I leave here I'll call my contact at the local precinct and have them track it down. At least we'll have a starting point tomorrow morning."

"Good. Now, you'd better get going. You're going to need some sleep too," I said.

"Hey Sam, don't worry. I'm sure we'll be able

to find May. And I'm going to put the precinct on stand-by, so that we can call them for help if we need to." When he saw my worried look, he added, "It's okay, we won't let Richard know. They'll be very discreet. I know some of the officers; we've collaborated on investigations before. They'll help us, and they'll keep quiet about it unless we need their presence."

"Fine, if you say so. I'll see you tomorrow at eight?" All of a sudden, I hated to see Fraser leave. I felt so alone, and powerless to help my father.

"Come here," Fraser said, taking hold of my arm and pulling me toward him. He enveloped me in a big bear hug. "I promise, it's going to be okay. We'll do everything in our power to make things turn out right."

"Thanks, Fraser. I couldn't bear it if my father lost May. She's all he's got."

"That's not true. He's got you, hasn't he?" he reminded me. "And whoever's got you, has got a force to be reckoned with," he tried to joke. He gave me a quick peck on the forehead and went out, closing the door behind him and walking quickly to his car.

Chapter Eleven

After Fraser left, I tidied the kitchen, washing and drying the few dishes we'd used and putting them away. Then I straightened the living room and let Mimi out for a quick run.

I decided I'd better get on the computer to Gabby before I went to bed—the next couple of days promised to be busy, and I might not get a chance. I unplugged the cord from the phone in the bedroom and plugged it into the computer. Turning on my e-mail program, I waited until the icon popped up to tell me that there was a message waiting.

Hi Sam, guess who? Well, I don't know about you but I'm having a great time. The weather over here is perfect, and I only have a couple

*of classes a day so I have lots of time to ex-
plore the area. I've been picking up some great
new recipes. Have you ever tried crêpes? They
are so delicious, and a specialty of the region.
I have managed to wheedle a recipe out of the
chef at one of the local eateries. He sprinkles
them with lemon and sugar or serves them with
strawberries and cream. Sometimes he even
stuffs them with seafood and serves them with
a delicious lemon sauce. Just wait until I come
home; you are going to love them. By the way,
I do feel a little homesick. Are you sure you
can't come over this summer? It would be
great to see you. Oh, I wanted to let you know
I'm leaving for Paris tomorrow instead of on
the weekend. There's some kind of holiday this
week, and the French have stretched it into a
four-day weekend, so Jean-Claude and I are
going to take off bright and early tomorrow.
Write back as soon as you get this, because I'll
be incommunicado after tomorrow morning,
and with the time difference, you might miss
me.*

Love, Gabby

She had made my mouth water with her description of crêpes. But unless I could figure out a way
to get over there this summer, I would have to wait
a whole year to try them. I sure missed her, and

Mimi missed Clem. The trip to Vancouver had helped Mimi forget that her friend was away, but once we got back to Victoria and Clem was nowhere to be seen, it would hit home again. And as for me, I had been so busy with this business of May's kidnapping that I had hardly had time to think about anything, never mind home. I clicked the reply button and began to write.

Gabby, glad you're enjoying your summer. It's been hectic here. I'm still at Richard and May's, though May is away temporarily. In the meantime, I'm cooking for Richard. Poor Richard, you say? Not so! I've made some great sandwiches. I may even try to dig up a recipe for crêpes. I wonder how they would taste stuffed with hamburger? Just kidding! Fraser popped over to Vancouver for a visit. We're trying to stay out of trouble. Enjoy your trip to Paris, but watch out for that Jean-Claude. There's something about him I don't like. I know I haven't met him, but I have this funny feeling, something I can't quite put my finger on. It must be my woman's intuition. Hey, I'm beginning to sound a lot like you! It's obviously time to say good-bye. Write again when you get back from Paris.

Cheers, Sam

I turned off the computer and put it away. Setting the alarm for seven o'clock, I climbed into the bed in the guest room, thinking I would never be able to sleep. But as soon as my head hit the pillow, I must have dozed off. The next thing I remember is hearing the alarm. Seven o'clock already? I woke up feeling as though I hadn't slept at all. I got up quickly, threw on my bathrobe, and went into the kitchen to start the coffee before calling Richard. There was no sound of him stirring yet. I decided to let him sleep a little longer. Taking a quick shower, I got dressed and went back into the kitchen to pour myself a cup of coffee. I poured one for Richard too, adding cream and sugar and carrying it to his room.

He was snoring lightly, and looked relaxed, the lines on his face having disappeared temporarily in sleep.

"Richard," I called softly.

"What?" he answered groggily, pulling himself up on one elbow and looking around. He was not yet fully awake.

"It's seven-thirty. I've brought you a cup of cof-fee."

"Sam—is everything okay?" He sat up. "Where's May?" he asked, then as he become more alert, he remembered the events of the previous day, and his whole demeanor changed. I watched as the worry lines reappeared on his forehead. "Anything new?" he asked fearfully, as if nervous to hear my answer.

"No, nothing," I said quickly. "Fraser should be here shortly. Why don't you drink your coffee, then get up and have a shower while I make us some breakfast?"

"Yes, all right," he agreed. "We have to find May, Sam; I can't take much more of this."

"We'll do our best," I promised, hoping our best would be good enough.

Fraser knocked on the door at eight exactly. He looked fresh and clean-shaven. I poured him some coffee, and he sat down at the kitchen table opposite Richard.

"I hope you managed to get a little sleep?" he asked Richard.

"Yes. I didn't think I would, but I did," Richard replied, trying to be polite, even he was obviously itching to get going. "What's the plan for this morning? I just hate to think of May spending more time than absolutely necessary in the company of that thug Patterson."

"Well, I've already called someone I know, and obtained the location of the pay phone Patterson called from yesterday. Do you know the Point Roberts area at all?"

"Yes," Richard said slowly. "I think so. I've been there once or twice, quite a few years ago. In fact,

I recall taking Sam and Martha there once with their mother. We had a picnic on the beach. This would have been when Sam was just a baby, mind you. I don't think I've been back to Point Roberts in almost 35 years. I don't suppose Sam would remember." He looked at me questioningly.

"Did you have to tell Fraser how old I am, Dad?" I teased. Then more seriously, "Point Roberts? Isn't it that small chunk of American soil just past Tsawwassen? Somewhat of an anomaly, if I remember correctly. A piece of the U.S. of A., surrounded by water on three sides and British Columbia on the fourth, with no land access to the rest of the States. I haven't been there since I was in my teens. But I *do* remember how to get there. I've noticed the directional signs when I've come off the ferry at Tsawwassen. I believe you turn at the second-to-last set of lights before the ferry. It shouldn't be too hard to find."

"That's where Patterson's call originated last night. It's not far, only a half-hour's drive from here. I suggest we finish our coffee and head down there. Apparently the pay phone is located at the local supermarket. I understand there's only one major grocery store on the Point, so it shouldn't be hard to find."

"Good idea. At least it's a fairly confined area. But I wonder how Patterson managed to get across the border. With his record, wouldn't he be stopped by the customs and immigration officials at the border crossing?"

"Only if they knew who he was. My contact tells me that the crossing is easy to traverse. Security is lax since most of the people going to the Point have summer cabins there, or are crossing from Tsawwassen just to buy gasoline, which is slightly cheaper across the line. Unless the border patrol had a reason to suspect who he was, they probably wouldn't even have stopped his car."

"Let's go. I just can't stand to sit idly by, while May is being held by Patterson," Richard said, getting up quickly. "Now that we know where to start looking, I want to get on with it."

We gathered up our things and got ready to leave. I put Richard's phone on call forward to my cell phone, in case there was a call from Patterson, though none of us thought he would phone again before midnight the next day. He had given Richard two days to come up with the money, and there really wouldn't be any point in his risking being found by placing another call.

Fraser said he wanted to drive, so we all piled into his car, Richard taking the back seat and me the one next to Fraser.

It was a short drive from Richard's, over the Arthur Laing Bridge and out River Road to Tsawwassen. River Road meandered beside the Fraser River, through an area where old boathouses and run-down homes shared space with a newly developed industrial park. Traffic was light, as most people had already arrived at work.

We skirted the town of Ladner and came to a set of traffic lights, where a sign indicated a left turn to Tsawwassen and Point Roberts. Traveling down 56th Street, we passed through a major shopping area, then started up a long, steep hill to the border.

Being mid-week and early in the morning, there was no line-up at the border crossing. We pulled up to the American customs building and a young man who didn't even look old enough to be working, never mind carrying the gun he had strapped to his hip, regarded us from his seat inside the booth.

"All Canadians?" he asked laconically.

"Yes," Fraser replied.

"Where y'all headed?"

"We're on vacation; just wanted to have a look around."

"Y'all have a nice day," he said as he waved us through.

The American side of the border didn't look much different than the Canadian side. Other than a road sign announcing a speed limit of 30 miles per hour rather than 50 kilometers, and an overabundance of American flags flying from flagpoles in front of the numerous gas stations dotting the route, a person might not know that they were in the United States. We drove straight ahead until we came to a four-way stop.

"Any of this look familiar?" Fraser asked.

"Nope. None of these gas stations were here the last time I was," I replied, looking around at the landscape. It was much too long since my previous visit and, although I wouldn't say that progress had caught up with this sleepy resort area, there were signs of new construction interspersed with derelict farmhouses and cottages along the route.

"I don't remember anything like this," Richard said. "I seem to recall that the border crossing was much closer to the water. I don't recognize a thing."

"Okay, let's just drive straight ahead and see if we can spot the supermarket."

It was a good decision. Within a few hundred yards, we saw first a sign that said *Point Roberts Marketplace*, and then, a little farther along, a large grocery store on the left. Fraser turned the car into the parking lot.

The most interesting thing about the store was the fact that almost all the cars outside it had B.C. plates. Apparently it was a Mecca for Canadian shoppers.

"Richard, you wait here in the car while Sam and I check things out."

"I'd like to come with you," Richard said.

"I know," Fraser replied patiently. "But what if

we bump into Patterson? He doesn't know me, but he'll surely recognize you."

"In that case, Sam had better stay here with me. She and Patterson met quite recently, so he's sure to remember who *she* is."

"You're right. You two stay here and I'll go alone and see if I can find the pay phone. I just want to make sure we're in the right spot."

Fraser turned off the ignition and got out of the car. He walked quickly to the store's entrance, and we lost sight of him. We sat silently, as if we'd all of a sudden run out of things to say. To me, it seemed that idle chitchat would be such an imposition under the circumstances, that it was better to remain quiet. I suspect it was the same for Richard. He gazed absently out the window.

Fraser returned in a few minutes. "This is the place all right. The pay phone is just inside the first set of doors, in a kind of alcove in front of the store entrance. I checked the number on the phone, and it's the same as on the call display last night."

"So we know Patterson was in this area last night. He must be holed up somewhere around here. What are we going to do next?" I asked. "I guess we could just drive around and see if we can spot the Ford. I have the licence number written down somewhere." I searched in my purse for my notebook.

"I picked up a brochure on the area, and the local newspaper, the *All Points Bulletin*. There's a map inside the brochure. I suggest we start at one end of the Point and drive up and down all the streets to see if we can find the car. It's not a huge area and much of it appears to be undeveloped. If Patterson is still around, we'll spot him."

"Okay, let's get started."

A few hours later, we had driven almost the entire Point, stopping only to grab a burger at a local pub at lunchtime, and we had not spotted the Ford. We had checked out the various areas around the Point, including Lighthouse Park, South Beach, and Maple Beach at the Boundary Bay end of the Point. In each area, we had seen small summer cabins interspersed with larger permanent homes, signs of a slowly changing time. There were Washington licence plates on a few vehicles parked in some driveways, but by far the majority of vehicles we saw were Canadian. There was no sign of the Ford.

Richard was exhausted and out of sorts with the strain of it all, and Fraser and I were feeling frustrated at our lack of progress. I suggested we take a short break. I had spotted a marina with a few-hundred boats moored at a series of docks. In one of the marina buildings, there was a small café. A sandwich board sign standing by the side of the road announced that it was open for business.

"Let's stop and have a coffee. Once we've had a break, I'm sure we'll get our second wind and we can finish checking the few remaining streets that we haven't already done."

Both men agreed. We parked in the small lot next to the café and went inside. There was only one other customer in the café, an attractive, though fading, blond who looked to be in her mid-forties. She looked up and smiled, then looked away, as we sat down not far from her.

The café was self-serve, so I asked Fraser and Richard what they wanted and went to the counter to order. The man behind the counter poured two mugs of coffee for Fraser and me and filled a small teapot with hot water for Richard. He put the drinks, along with a couple of pastries, on a plastic tray. I carried the tray back to our table, passing by the blond. On closer inspection, she looked older than I had first thought, her face tanned and leathery, as though she spent too much time in the wind and sun. She glanced at me curiously, then went back to eating her plate of fish and chips.

"What next?" Richard asked. He looked completely crushed, as though all the spark had gone out of him. The stressful situation was taking its toll. May was younger than Richard and by far the spunkier of the two, I had noticed, even before this incident. I hoped she was handling the situation better than he was.

"We'll finish our search. If we don't find anything, we're going home, and you're going to lie down," I said to Richard. "You look positively grey. Fraser and I will continue the search on our own."

"I am exhausted," he confessed. "I don't know how much more of this I can take."

"Drink your coffee and eat one of these." I handed him a pastry, and he took a uninterested bite of it.

The blond woman had finished her early dinner. She got up from the table, stopping to talk to the fellow behind the counter for a moment before going out the door. She disappeared around the corner of the building, and it crossed my mind that she must live on one of the boats. That would explain the tan.

We paid our bill and went back to the car. As we were about to pull out of the parking lot, I spotted a car in the distance, speeding away from the marina.

"Hey, isn't that the Ford? Hurry up, Fraser, step on it. Don't lose it!" I leaned forward to get a better look.

The vehicle was several hundred yards away, too far for me to be able to read the licence plate. Fraser got out onto the road from the parking area and accelerated, changing gears and getting up to cruising speed. The Ford was still quite far ahead.

It stopped at the corner and turned left, traveling back toward the grocery store where the pay phone that Patterson had used to call Richard was located.

We followed, not even worrying about being spotted, since we were far enough back not to be recognized. The Ford signaled and turned into the grocery store parking area, stopping at a parking stall near the door. The driver got out of the vehicle as we drove into the lot. We parked in the first available spot, concealing ourselves behind a truck situated between Fraser's car and the Ford. I jumped out of the car and, hiding behind the truck, tried to catch a better look at the driver.

The woman from the coffee shop! She was the last person I expected to see. I must admit I felt as deflated as a punctured balloon. I had been so sure it would be Patterson. The woman disappeared inside the store. As soon as the door closed behind her, I walked over to the car and checked the licence plate. It was definitely Patterson's vehicle. So who was the lady, and why was she driving Patterson's car?

Back at Fraser's car, the two men were waiting impatiently.

"Well?" Fraser asked.

"It's Patterson's Ford all right, but he's not driving it. It's the blond woman from the café. She's gone inside. I think we should wait until she comes out and see where she goes."

Fraser and I discussed possible scenarios while we waited for the woman to return to the car. As we were arguing about what to do next, a man and woman came out of the store, pushing a shopping cart. They came straight over to the truck parked next to us. They loaded their groceries into the back, all the while watching us curiously. We returned their stares. When they finally drove away, we had an unobstructed view of where the Ford had been. I say *where it had been* because it was no longer there. While we had been watching the people in the truck and they us, we had neglected to keep an eye on the Ford, and it had somehow slipped out of the lot without our noticing.

Richard was speechless with disappointment. It was all too much for him. He sat there numbly, while Fraser and I discussed what to do next.

"I think we should take Richard home. From there we can try and figure out our next move," I said.

Fraser agreed, and Richard didn't protest so I knew he must be completely done in. Before he could say anything we drove quickly to the border. The Canadian customs officer asked only how long we had been at the Point and whether we were bringing any goods back with us. When we said *no*, he waved us through.

Chapter Twelve

We arrived back at Richard's in just over an hour, though the traffic was beginning to heat up with rush-hour approaching. As soon as we arrived, Richard went to lie down, while Fraser and I settled ourselves at the kitchen table.

"What are we going to do?" I asked.

"First things first. Is there anyone who can come and stay with your father?" Fraser asked. "I don't think he can handle much more running around. And we would be able to move faster without having to worry about him."

"I'll call my sister Martha right now. I'm sure she can get Mum to watch Timmy while she comes over here. She'll want to help, once she knows what has happened."

"Okay, why don't you do that while I make a couple of calls?" He pulled out his cell phone and went into the living room.

I dialed Martha's number. When she replied, I quickly explained the situation, telling her I'd fill in the blanks when she arrived. She said she'd call the heliport and see if she could get a spot on the next flight. That was the fastest way to get off the Island and to Vancouver. I suggested she get a cab to Richard's when she landed, and we'd see her as soon as she could make it. By the time I got off the phone, Fraser was back in the kitchen.

"Okay, here's what we need to do," he said. He proceeded to explain how he thought we should use the time we had left, before we could expect to hear from Patterson again. I didn't really like letting him take the lead, but I couldn't disagree with his plan, especially since he didn't try to shut me out of it.

He said we needed to locate Patterson. I couldn't disagree with that. He proposed that he and I return to the Point and try to find the Ford. There were still a few places we hadn't looked. If we could find out for sure that Patterson was at Point Roberts, it would make the rest of our planning easier. The idea was that when Patterson called, Richard would set up a meeting for the following night. Fraser would arrange to be close by with a bunch of his uniformed friends, whose presence would remain a secret between Fraser and me.

I would go back to Point Roberts and stake out Patterson's hideout, assuming we found it. Once Patterson left the Point to go to the rendezvous with Richard, I would somehow get into the hideout, find May, get her out of there, and come back across the border. Everything hinged on Patterson and May being somewhere on the Point, and on us finding out where. And that's what Fraser and I would do, while Martha stayed with Richard.

There was one other thing I wanted to do, and that was to return to Mary Lucas's apartment to see if I could enlist her help. Fraser thought it was a dumb idea, but that's because he doesn't understand women any more than most other men. I was sure that Mary would be more than a little upset when I told her about the blond that we'd seen driving Patterson's car. Even though I had no idea what their relationship actually was—Patterson and the blond, I mean—even a hint of a more-than-friendship between them would likely have the effect of changing Mary's allegiance. It had been apparent, from our previous meeting, that the relationship was already on rocky ground and that she was beginning to doubt the wisdom of her decision to let him move in. Hardly any woman I knew would countenance his behavior, never mind Mary who seemed as straight as an arrow. I was counting also on Mary knowing something about Bob's activities, though I hadn't thought things through enough to decide what. If anyone could help us pin down his location, it could be she.

Fraser agreed to wait at Richard's for Martha to arrive, while I went to the apartment building on Salisbury Street for a heart-to-heart with Mary.

The lights were on in the apartment, and the Ford was missing from the parking lot. Conditions were perfect for a quick visit. I parked in front of the building and walked up to the door, pushing the button for apartment 303 on the intercom panel. Mary Lucas answered immediately.

"Hello, Mary, this is Sam Hope. I don't know if you remember me?" I asked, my fingers crossed that she would recall us having been introduced by Helga Jackson.

"Sam, yes, of course I do. Come on up."

The buzzer sounded and I grabbed for the door and slipped inside. Once my eyes adjusted to the glare from the late afternoon sun hitting the red and gold walls, I punched the *up* arrow to call the elevator and waited for it to arrive.

The hallway on the third floor was empty. Walking quickly to Mary Lucas's apartment, I knocked, and the door opened.

"Hi Sam. What brings you to this area? Visiting Helga again?" Mary asked. Her smile, though not open and relaxed, was welcoming.

"Actually I came to see you. Can I come in for a moment?"

"Certainly." She stood aside to let me pass. "How about that cup of tea I promised you last time you were here?"

"That would be nice. I only have a short time though."

"I was just boiling the kettle when you rang, so it will only take a moment." She left me in the living room and went into the kitchen to make the tea.

"You didn't say what brought you to the area, Sam," she called from the kitchen.

"Bob Patterson," I said.

She came back into the living room, her face grim, and set a tray with two mugs of steaming tea and containers of cream and sugar on the coffee table in front of the sofa. "What about Bob?" The look on her face told me that she already suspected something was amiss.

"I know it's none of my business, but I just wondered if you knew about his lady friend? I happened to see him at Point Roberts earlier today with a good-looking blond. It made my blood boil to think that he might be two-timing you, after all you've done for him."

"Point Roberts! He told me he was going to visit an old buddy who had a boat moored at the Point. And I thought his friend was a man," she said, disgusted with herself for having been duped, and with him for being such a creep, I expect. "Of all the nerve!"

She pretended anger, but the look in her eyes was pure hurt. She *had* done a lot for him, both while he was in prison and since, and all he'd done for her was give her a big headache.

"Did he happen to say what the name of the boat was or where it was moored?"

"No, I don't think so. No, hold on, I think he said the boat was called Blondie—I remember wondering if it was named after the comic strip character. And I think he said it was moored at the marina. Is there more than one marina down there, do you know?"

"I think there's just one; the Point Roberts Marina; but I'm not absolutely sure." Blondie! The boat must have been named after the woman who'd been driving Patterson's car. That pointed to a relationship of longer standing between them. "Are you expecting him back here tonight, Mary?"

"I was, but after what you've told me, not any more. Now that I think of it, he *was* acting kind of strange when he left. He was all excited, just like a kid—said something about buried treasure. I think he'd been drinking. He took a duffel bag with him. I just assumed he and his friend were going fishing and he needed a change of clothes. Now, I don't think he was planning to come back. What an idiot I've been!"

"If I were you, I would change the lock on the door," I said, thinking that good old Bob could become violent if he did return and she confronted him with his possible infidelity. From all that Richard had said about him, he wasn't exactly a nice, mild-mannered fella.

"You're right, of course. You know, I never thought it would come to this," she said, looking sad. "I've been such a silly old fool. I really thought he meant to change his ways."

"Don't be too hard on yourself, Mary. You're just too nice for your own good. Now what about calling the super and seeing if you can get the lock changed tonight. I'm nervous for you. I don't want to leave you here alone."

"Don't worry, I'll be fine. I'm tougher than I look." She smiled, putting on a brave face.

It was hard to walk away and leave her to deal with the aftermath of Patterson's betrayal, but I had to get going. Now that I had a good idea where Patterson was holed up, I wanted to go back to the Point with Fraser and see if we could find the two *Blondies*. Locating the boat was crucial to my being prepared to carry out my part of our plan the following night.

Martha was as good as her word. She must have caught the helijet almost as soon as we had got off the phone because it wasn't more than an hour, give or take, after I got back to Richard's from Mary's that we heard a vehicle outside, and looked out to see a taxi pulling into the driveway.

Richard had just gotten up from a nap feeling more rested and alert than earlier. When he found out what we were planning he started to protest at being excluded, but gave up once he realized that Fraser and I had things more or less under control and that he needed to save his strength for the final showdown with Patterson the following night.

I introduced Martha and Fraser. From that point on, she raised her eyebrows each time she caught my eye. I could tell she was dying to ask me all about him, but our sisterly tête-à-tête would have to wait. We only had time to fill her in on what had happened to May, leaving Richard to go over the finer points with her. Fraser and I headed for the Point, promising to check in with them if we found out where May was being held.

Traffic being what it is during rush hour, our half-hour trip to the border stretched to an hour and a half. I thought to myself that if we continued to cross back and forth regularly, the guard would begin to suspect us of smuggling. But they must have changed shifts since our previous trip across because a tall African-American man with a strong Southern accent was on duty at the booth. He asked the same questions as the young fellow we had encountered earlier and elicited the same answers. He

ushered us through the crossing with hardly a backward glance.

"Okay, what do we do now?" I asked Fraser, who
stopped briefly at the four way stop, then crossed
through it, heading straight toward the marina.

"We find ourselves a good spot where we can
keep an eye on the boats and we check if the Ford
is parked in the marina parking lot. Then we wait
for Patterson to show up. It would be a real bonus
if we managed to catch a glimpse of May. Then
we'd know for sure that Patterson was hiding her
on the *Blondie*."

Fraser drove past the parking lot and around the
block. It being the beginning of summer, there were
dozens of cars in the carpark, and lots of activity
on the numerous jetties. At least we wouldn't have
to worry about looking out of place. We would
blend in with the vacationers.

Parking the car at the far end of the lot, we got
out and walked along the waterfront. A pretty land-
scaped path meandered along the water's edge, next
to a tall chain-link fence that was supposed to keep
out intruders. With a couple of strands of razor wire
stretched across the top, it was probably successful.

We walked along the path and watched as people
went in and out of the various gates that led to the
piers where the boats were moored, opening the
gates by punching in a code on a large keypad.

"That will be your biggest challenge, Sam," Fraser said, pointing to the gates. "You'll have to find a way to get hold of the code, or else find some obliging person to let you in. Other than the fence and gates though, there doesn't appear to be any other security."

"Piece of cake," I said, wondering how the heck I was supposed to do it. I would have to find a way, that's all there was to it. "No problemo!" I said, with more confidence than I felt.

"Let's wander down toward that gate over there," Fraser said, pointing to one of the locked gates a short distance away. "We need to figure out which boat is Patterson's."

No sooner had we arrived at the gate than we heard the crunch of someone walking on gravel behind us. That someone was coming up the path, heading our way. Fraser grabbed me and pulled me into a steamy embrace, bringing his lips down hard on mine. My head started to swim.

"Pretend you're enjoying this, Sam," he whispered urgently. "I don't want the woman to see your face."

I could see nothing, but from what he said, I assumed that it must be Blondie approaching. And I didn't have to pretend either. He had caught me off-guard, and his kiss rocked me from my head right down to my high-top sneakers. But just when I started to respond, he pulled back, leaving me standing there gasping like a dying fish.

"Sorry, I had to think fast. She's gone now." He said casually, as if the kiss had not affected him in the least. Then he winked, and I knew he was just pulling my chain. What a cheap trick!

I turned to follow his gaze, which was focused on the dock below us. Patterson's lady was making her way purposefully down the creaking boards of the pier to a large sailboat at the end of the pier.

It was a beautiful sleek craft, at least forty feet long, sitting low in the water, like a racer hunched over waiting for the starter's gun. A small ramp enabled the woman to climb easily onto the boat from the pier. She climbed in and swung herself on board.

"Stay right here. I just remembered I have a small pair of binoculars in the car. I'll be right back," Fraser said. He turned and headed off toward the car.

I continued to watch the boat. The woman was no longer visible. She had gone below. The boat swayed gently in the water, but other than the slight movement, there was no sign that it was occupied.

Fraser came hurrying back along the path and handed me the binoculars. Adjusting them to my eyes, I turned them on the boat. No one was around. We would begin to lose the light soon. I hoped we would spot someone before long.

There was a bench nearby, so I suggested to Fraser that we sit down and keep an eye on the boat from there. He agreed.

It had dawned on me earlier that we never did find out from Richard where Patterson said the money was hidden, so I asked Fraser what he thought we should do. "Do you think that we should check out the spot where the money from the robbery is supposed to have been hidden?" I asked as we sat waiting for some sign of activity down below.

"It might be helpful. Actually it might work to have the meeting between Richard and Patterson take place there, depending on where it is. Richard could tell Patterson he had found the money and hidden it again close by. If we have an opportunity to check out the spot, we could alert the police and they could begin to plan how they wanted to be positioned to observe the meeting. Why don't you call him and find out?"

I dialed Richard's number. After two or three rings, Martha answered.

"It's me, Sam," I said.

"Sam, how are things going? Is everything all right?" she asked, her tone one of concern.

"Just peachy," I replied. "How's Dad?"

"Better. He has calmed down and he's sitting reading the paper at the moment. Do you want to talk to him?"

"Yes please; I have to ask him something."

"Hang on a minute, I'll call him."

Richard came on the line. "Sam, Martha said you wanted to talk to me. Did you find May?" His voice was hopeful.

"Not yet," I admitted, not wanting to say anything about having found the boat until we knew for sure that Patterson was actually on it. "But we won't give up. I'm sure she's here somewhere. Actually Fraser and I were just wondering where Patterson told you he hid the robbery money."

"Oh, right. I forgot to tell you earlier. We were going to go there and check it out. With all the goings-on, I'm feeling a little flustered," he admitted.

"Don't worry," I reassured. "I forgot about it myself until just now. We wouldn't mind stopping there on our way back to your place later, after we're finished here."

"Well, it's not hard to find. You know where Central Park is? You go into the park by a trail at the southeast corner. There's a public restroom in the area. You'll see a gazebo, where people go with their picnic lunches. Patterson said just behind the gazebo, there was a big, old stump. He said he buried the money in a plastic bag on the north side of the stump between it and the gazebo. He said that when he went back the stump was gone and so was the money. I've never bothered to go and check out the area."

"Thanks, Dad." I hung up the phone and turned to Fraser. "Patterson hid the money at Central Park in Burnaby. Let's go there as soon as we're finished here."

"I only hope we can get away from here before dark. Hey, what's that?" Fraser sat up straighter and looked sharply in the direction of the boat. "Give me the binoculars."

I handed him the glasses, and he studied the boat intently. "There's someone up on deck. Take a look and tell me if you can make out who it is." He handed the binoculars back to me.

"It's Patterson. I'd recognize that big, ugly mug anywhere. Wait! Someone else is coming out of the cabin. It's May, and the blond is right behind her. They haven't got her tied up or anything."

I handed the binoculars back to Fraser, and he took another look. "So that's Patterson. And May. That's what we needed to know. She looks okay. I guess they are not too worried about her escaping, with the two of them watching her."

"I wish we could just storm down there and grab her, but I know we can't take the chance," I said regretfully. At least we know she's alive and un-harmed."

"Let's get out of here. You can call your father from the car and let him know you've seen her."

He grabbed my hand, and we walked quickly back to the car and sped away.

Chapter Thirteen

"Let's see if we can make it to Central Park before dark. Do you know where it is?" Fraser asked, after we had gone back through the border and I had called Richard to let him know about seeing May.

"Yes, I lived in Burnaby while I was going to the university. It's right on the border between Burnaby and Vancouver. The park stretches for quite a distance. From what Richard said, Patterson buried the money in the southeast corner. So we should head toward the Knight Street Bridge and follow Marine Drive to Boundary Road. If we go north on Boundary to Imperial, we'll hit the southwest corner of the park, then we just have to turn right on Imperial and—"

"Hold on, you can direct me as we go; I'll never remember all of that," Fraser said.

The light was fading fast as we arrived at the park. We parked on Imperial and walked back, entering the park at the southeast corner as Richard had suggested. I spotted a square cement building not far away and figured that must be the public washroom. We headed in that direction.

"I don't see any gazebo, do you?" I asked Fraser. He shook his head.

"I wonder if there is any security in the park," he said.

"Why?"

"I was thinking if there's someone working around here, we could ask where the gazebo is. It could save us a lot of time."

"You're right. Let's try the washroom. If there isn't anyone there, there's also a pitch and putt golf course a short distance away. We might have better luck there."

There was no one around the washroom—no security, that is. The building appeared to be a meeting place for those in search of close, albeit temporary, companionship. We waded our way through the lewd and suggestive comments of the locals and got out of the area as quickly as possible.

"So that's how the other half lives," I joked to Fraser.

"You don't know the half of it," he replied. "Remind me to tell you a few stories some time."

"I can hardly wait. Let's go over to the pitch and putt course. There's a sign over there. I pointed to an intersection in the trail, where it met with another running east and west. It indicated that the golf course was located at the west end of the trail.

"This is crazy; we really can't see well enough to find anything here tonight."

"Let's at least talk to someone this evening, that is, if we can find anyone. If we learn anything, we'll come back again early tomorrow before the park gets busy," Fraser suggested.

We found the pitch and putt course and the attendant, who was in the process of packing up and getting ready to leave. Fraser asked him if he knew the area well.

"I ought to; I've worked here off and on for ten years," he replied.

"Do you know about a gazebo in this part of the park?" I asked.

"Sure, but it's gone now. It was torched by some kids a couple of years ago. The parks department never bothered to replace it. It was just over there." He pointed in the direction we had come from. "Where you turned west to come over here, you should have turned east. It was near the edge of the park, close to Imperial Street."

"Thanks for your help," I said. And to Fraser,

"Let's try once more to find it, before it gets any darker. We might be able to spot some debris or something to give us an idea where it used to be."

"Okay, but hurry up. We don't have much time."

We raced back along the trail, turning right at the crossroad, and heading toward where we had entered the park. I noticed a small clearing up ahead, where there were no large trees, just low bushes and grass.

"I'll bet that's the spot," I told Fraser, as we broke through from the forested path into the clearing.

We walked all around the area, searching the ground. Finally Fraser bent over and picked up a piece of burnt wood.

"This is it." He looked around, scoping out the area for suitability for the meeting between Richard and Patterson. "This might work as a meeting place too. There's lots of cover for police backup. And it's close to the road. I'm going to talk to the guys as soon as we get out of here."

I had wandered off to one side of the clearing in search of the big stump Richard had mentioned.

"Hey, look at this!" I pointed to a depression in the ground. "Doesn't this look like perhaps a stump was blasted or dug out of here? I'll bet this is where the money was hidden. Too bad it's so dark. We have to come back here tomorrow and have a closer look. Do you have a shovel in your car?" I asked, never thinking for a moment the answer would be yes.

"As a matter of fact, I do. I used to be a Boy Scout, you know. I'm prepared for just about anything." He laughed sheepishly.

"Hey, I'm not knocking it. It might be nice to be around someone who's more organized than I am for a change," I said, glad he couldn't see the blush that started to creep from my neck up to my face. I was thinking he might interpret my words to mean that we would be spending time together after we got Richard through this ordeal. I didn't want to be the one to stick my neck out and expose my feelings. Somehow that felt even more dangerous than a late-night encounter with Patterson.

We headed for the car. Fraser asked me to drive, so he could get on the phone with his friend from the precinct. He explained to him what had happened since they had spoken the night before and asked him to arrange for backup the following night. The local police were most interested in the possibility of recovering the stolen money and warmed to the plan. We promised to keep in touch as things developed, and to let him know if Richard was able to convince Patterson to meet him at the park.

Fraser dropped me off at Richard's. He didn't bother to come in, saying it was late and we'd have to be up early the next day. We had a lot of ground to cover and preparations to make, before the meeting with Patterson the next night.

I set the alarm for seven once again, and, after giving Richard and Martha a report, went to bed. I told them I would try not to awaken them when I got up early to go with Fraser to the park, and that I'd be back by noon to prepare for the following night's activities.

Fraser was as good as his word. Once again, he arrived at the house before eight, and after a hasty cup of coffee and whispered conversation in the kitchen we headed back to Central Park. We parked as close as possible to the area where we had found the remains of the gazebo the night before. Fraser locked the car and took the shovel out of the trunk, and we set off to scope out the potential meeting site in daylight.

The nightlife had all gone home to bed—the park was deserted except for the occasional jogger. There was no one to disturb us, as we made our way through the woods to the clearing.

There was no doubt that this was where the gazebo had stood a few years back. Fraser checked the area to see if he could find anything interesting, while I wandered back to the depression that I had found the night before. It definitely looked as though a large stump had been removed from the spot. The depression was about the size of some of the larger tree trunks in the vicinity, and there were a few pieces of rotting tree root strewn about on the ground. I recalled Richard having said that the money had been buried between the gazebo and stump, so I began to make a thorough search of the ground between the two spots.

It was not surprising that Patterson thought someone had taken his money. It looked as though the area may have changed considerably with the stump having been removed, and the gazebo burning down. It was little wonder he hadn't been able to find it. I had to walk the area several times myself before I finally spotted something.

A small piece of plastic on the ground caught the light and stood out like a tiny beacon, drawing me to the spot. I leaned over to pick it up and found that it was partially buried. I couldn't get it to budge, even when I tugged at it as hard as I could. The plastic tore and I was left holding a small piece in my hand, while the rest remained underground. I hollered at Fraser to bring the shovel.

"What have you got there?" he asked, handing me the small folding shovel.

"It's probably just someone's garbage, but it bears further investigation, I think. Do you want to dig, or should I?" I asked, hoping he would volunteer.

"You go ahead. I want to make a sketch of the area, so I can pass it on to the police team that will be on duty tonight." He wandered off in the direction of the public toilets.

I unfolded the handle of the shovel and started using it to poke at the plastic, to see if I could loosen it from the dirt. It wouldn't move so I began to dig. After removing a couple of shovels of dirt, I hit a rock. It seemed that a large flat rock had been placed over the plastic, and it was trapped underneath. So that was why I hadn't been able to pull the whole piece of plastic out of the dirt.

"Fraser, I don't want to be a wimp, but I need your help," I called when I wasn't able to lift the rock on my own.

"Hang on a minute, I'll be right there."

He took his own sweet time about coming to help. By the time he drifted over, I had loosened the rock by removing the dirt all around it. But I still couldn't get it off the ground; it was just too heavy.

"Okay, let's see what you've got here," he said. He bent over and tried to move the rock.

"It's going to take the two of us, I think," I said sweetly, thinking to myself, *if it was that easy, buddy, I would have picked it up with one hand and tossed it like a discus*. I bent my knees and got ready to lift. "Ready? Heave!"

We both lifted at the same time, and the rock came loose and was lifted high enough off the ground to be shifted to one side. Now the plastic bag was fully exposed.

"Hmm, interesting!" I said.

I pulled at the bag, and it crumbled in my hands. As it broke apart, several bundles of Canadian bills, twenties and fifties mostly, fell out of it.

"Do they still have that rule about finders-keepers?" I asked, grinning from ear to ear.

"You found it! Good work, Sam," Fraser said, giving me a hug. "I think I've got an old duffel bag in the car; I'll go get it, and we can load the money into it."

We made short work of the job. I was afraid someone would come along and see us, but the park was still quiet. We finished removing the money from the hole, filled it up with dirt and carried the duffel bag and shovel back to the car.

"Now, Sam, I think we should avoid mentioning the money to the local police for the time being," Fraser warned. "I want to stop by the police station and talk to them about our plans for tonight, but I don't want to tell them we found the loot. Just in case things don't go as we planned, this money is our *ace in the hole*. My first priority is making sure that May gets home in one piece."

"Hey, I noticed you didn't answer my question about finders-keepers. I'm all for keeping the money a secret . . . forever," I said, dreaming for a moment about all the things I could do with $250,000.

"Sam, you know that's not possible," Fraser admonished.

"Hey, a woman can dream, can't she?"

We stopped at the police station on the way back to Richard's. I waited in the car while Fraser went inside. I needed time to think about how I was going to get through or over that chain-link fence at the marina to rescue May. If I didn't find some obliging soul to open the gate for me, I needed to be ready to climb over the fence or snip it apart. Anything to gain access. I knew for sure that my usual tricks wouldn't work; there was no point in hauling out the grey wig and flowered dress. I had to come up with a better idea.

A short time later Fraser came back to the car and, as we drove to Richard's, he told me what he had set up with the police. They would go to the area well in advance of the meeting time, whatever that turned out to be, roust the locals, and take over the washroom. They would be dressed to look like they were there for *a good time, not a long time* as the saying goes. There would be additional officers stationed wherever there was cover, including at the pitch and putt course. Since the meeting would likely take place late at night, they should have no problem making themselves invisible if they dressed in black.

We had no plans to tell Richard about the police presence. He would only need to know that Fraser would be stationed nearby when he went to meet Patterson. And, if he and Fraser got the call from me that I had managed to free May, he might not have to meet Patterson at all.

Chapter Fourteen

We held a final strategy meeting at Richard's that afternoon. Fraser outlined the plan to Richard and Martha. Richard was overjoyed to learn that we had managed to recover the robbery money from its cache and planned to hold it in reserve, so that it would be available in the unhappy event that I was unable to free May from the hiding place where Patterson had her.

Once Richard settled down, he was very calm and composed about the prospective meeting. Knowing how he felt about Patterson, I was suspicious about what he might be planning himself, but I kept quiet and waited to see how things developed.

Martha demanded and got a role as the chief dispatcher.

"Just because I'm not a P.I. like my illustrious sister doesn't mean that I can't cut the mustard," she insisted.

Fraser and Richard agreed, so I had to go along with it. It wasn't that I minded her being involved. As long as her role was a passive one that didn't put her in any danger, it was okay by me. It was just that I was godmother to her son, Timmy, and considered myself totally unfit to take over his care and upbringing should anything happen to her.

But I knew Martha had to be involved. It had taken considerable convincing to get her to agree to meet with Richard, once I had found and been re-united with him myself. Now that she had, they had developed a close relationship based on their mutual love for Tim, Richard's only grandchild.

After the meeting adjourned, the rest of the day passed quickly; however, a somber mood descended on the house as we prepared to go our separate ways. I dressed in dark clothing, which put me more or less in my usual wardrobe, and made sure that my cell phone was charged and ready for use. I put some wire cutters in the car along with a pair of heavy work gloves. One way or another I would master the fence and get into the inside compound, to gain access to the sailboat where May was being held.

Martha had prepared dinner so we ate it, though no one had much of an appetite. As night fell, we all became restless and tense. Each of us showed it in his or her own way. Martha started baking cookies. I just paced up and down; no point doing anything useful. Richard sat in his chair, his hand on the phone, waiting for Patterson's call.

It finally came about ten o'clock. Richard answered the phone, while Fraser listened once again on the kitchen extension.

"Howell, have you got the money?"

As planned, Richard told him that he did. He asked Patterson where he wanted to meet him.

"How about I come by your place and pick it up?" Patterson asked, his tone nasty.

"No way; I'll tell *you* what you're going to do. Go to Central Park, to the spot where you had the money hidden. And bring May with you. You're not getting the money until I get her back, you hear me?"

There was total silence on the other end of the line. Finally Patterson said, "I'll meet you there at one, three hours from now. But no way I'm bringing May with me. No way!" he repeated emphatically. "I want the money first. I plan to count every penny of it before I let her go. Don't worry; if you're playing straight with me, I won't hurt her."

"Why should I trust you?" Richard asked.

"Why should *I* trust *you*? Where did you get the money anyway?" Patterson asked.

"Never mind. That's none of your business. All

you need to know is that I've got it. That's all that counts."

"Okay," he said grudgingly. "Like I said, I'll meet you in three hours. And come alone. No cops. If you play straight with me, you'll be reunited with the little lady before morning. If not . . ."

Patterson left the sentence hanging in an unfinished threat. Reluctantly Richard agreed to his demands. He knew that I was going to do everything in my power to get her off the boat as soon as Patterson left Point Roberts, so he wasn't overly insistent. Besides, even though we had the money, Patterson had May, so he still had the upper hand.

Richard hung up, and Fraser came back into the living room. "Okay, that was good, Richard. That went exactly as we planned. Now, I'm going to be at the park at about midnight. You come along a little later; don't get there until just before one. You should arrive just before Patterson if possible, though it will be hard to gauge exactly when that is. We have to assume that he'll come at one o'clock. You won't be able to see me, but I'll be there. When you arrive at the park, station yourself just off Imperial Street at the southeast corner of the park, just far enough into the woods to be out of the streetlights. Here's a flashlight. I've put new batteries in it. And I've got one just like it. When I see you arrive, I'll turn mine off and on a couple of times to let you know where I am."

"Okay, I think I've got it straight," Richard said nervously. "You'll be there before me. You'll flash the flashlight when you see me. Then all I have to do is wait for Patterson to show up."

"Right," Fraser said. "Sam, you'd better get going. When you get to the marina, call me on the cell phone. I'll have the ringer turned off, but I'll be able to feel it vibrate. I want to know as soon as Patterson leaves the Point. That will give us an idea of what time he'll be arriving at Central Park."

"Yes sir," I said, saluting cheekily.

"Sam, this is no joke," Fraser warned, a stern look on his otherwise handsome face.

"Haven't you figured out yet that's how I handle stress?" I replied. "Well, I'm off. I'll check in with you in about an hour."

Since Martha was staying behind as dispatch, all of us had orders to check in with her from time to time. If we had a problem we were to contact her immediately and she would act as a clearing-house, letting each of us know what was happening. If she didn't hear from us by two, she had surreptitious orders from Fraser to call the police.

"I'm off then, wish me luck," I said, all of a sudden feeling the butterflies stampeding around in my stomach. Why is it that I always feel fine right up to the moment of departure, and then all hell breaks loose inside me?

I gave Richard a hug, whispering to him not to

try anything foolish. He gave me a look that spoke volumes. I wanted to warn Fraser to keep an eye on him but didn't get a chance, and later when I had the opportunity, I totally forgot.

"I'll walk you to your van," Fraser said.

We went outside, and Fraser opened the door of the van. Always the gentleman, I thought. I got in and closed it, rolling down the window.

"Sam, promise me you'll be careful. We have no idea what you're going to be facing on that boat, or even if you will somehow be able to get through the gate."

"I know. Don't worry, I'll get in, and I'll get out again, with May," I said, with much more confidence than I felt. "I'll call you shortly."

"Take care," he said, and reached up to give me a quick kiss, holding on a little longer and tighter than necessary. "I'll see you soon." He started to walk away.

"Fraser, you take care too," I called after him. "I'm getting real used to having you around. Don't go acting silly and getting yourself hurt."

He gave me one of his devilish grins as he turned to go back into the house, and I felt a momentary panic that I might lose him so soon after we had found each other. *Pull yourself together, Sam,* I thought, as I put the van into reverse and backed out of the driveway. *He's a professional, remember? You just concentrate on staying out of trouble.*

* * *

The trip to the border was uneventful. The only problem I had was in feeling left out of the action. Since I was going to the Point by myself and would be alone until I managed to rescue May, I wouldn't know what the others were up to. I would have preferred to be going to the park with Richard and Fraser. But my part in the plan was, in a way, the most important. The main idea of the whole operation was to get May away from Patterson and back to Richard, unharmed. Success or failure of the mission rested with me.

There were a few cars lined up at the American customs and immigration. I waited impatiently until it was my turn to go through. The young man who had been on duty the first time we'd crossed the line was back on duty. He didn't recognize me, and didn't even bother to ask where I was going or where I was from. He just took a look at me, flicked his hand, and waved me through.

I headed straight for the marina, glad that at least I knew where I was going this time. If I'd had to find my way there for the first time in the dark it would have been much more difficult. As it was, I missed a turn and ended up on the wrong side of the marina near the coffee shop where we had first seen Blondie. I did a U-turn and went back toward the parking lot on the other side. Once I found a spot, I checked the lot to see if I could see the Ford.

There it was, close to the gate where I soon expected to see Patterson exiting.

I called Fraser and reported in.

"Everything okay?" he asked.

"Yes, I'm parked a few cars away from the Ford. I haven't seen Patterson yet. It's dark, and I can't make out much, but there are lights on the boat, so I guess he's here. I'll call again when he leaves, just before I make my way down to the jetty."

"Right, and Sam, take it slow. Don't do anything stupid."

"Moi? Surely you jest?" I joked. "Talk to you later," I said and hung up. The nerve!

I glanced at my watch. It was eleven-thirty. Patterson would have to leave the Point soon if he was going to make it to Central Park on time. I got out of the car and locked the door. The trouble was, I couldn't see the boat from where I was situated, only the Ford. I had to get closer to the gate, where I could keep an eye on both the car and the sailboat without being seen either by other passersby or by Patterson. I crept closer to the gate, crouching down behind a sports utility vehicle. It wasn't too likely that I would have to worry about anyone coming along at this time of night. In fact, now that I saw how deserted it was, I was wondering what my chances would be of finding someone to let me in the gate.

Suddenly I heard voices. The sound carried well

across the water and through the quiet night air. I could make out almost every word.

"Okay, Bobby, I'll be ready. What time did you say you'd be back?"

"Between two-thirty and three. Have the boat ready to go, okay? I don't want to hang around once I've got the money. We're almost there, honey. Don't let me down."

"I won't. I can hardly wait to get out of this place, and back into the sun. I'll see you in a little while."

Patterson! He was on his way from the boat to the end of the jetty. He just had to climb the long ramp to the gate and he'd be almost in front of me, and on his way to the rendezvous. I couldn't see him once he started up the ramp but I *could* hear the heavy thud of his footsteps. I crouched down lower, out of sight of him and the Ford. I heard the clang of the metal gate as he opened and shut it after himself. Then I heard the car door as he opened and closed it. He started the engine and backed out of the parking spot.

I crept around to the front of the vehicle I was hiding beside, so that I wouldn't be caught in Patterson's headlights like a deer on the highway. He revved the engine and drove off. As soon as he was out of sight, I pulled out the cell phone and punched in Fraser's number.

"Sam?" Fraser asked.

"Yeah. Patterson just left the marina. I heard him

talking to the blond. They're planning to sail south as soon as he gets back with the money."

"Okay, thanks. Are you going over the fence now?"

"I thought I'd wait for a few minutes and see if anyone comes along. I'm not too hopeful though; it's pretty quiet here. What's happening there?"

"I've just arrived at the park. I'm going to rendezvous with the police, then get into position before your father arrives. Call me back in a half hour and let me know what's happening, okay?"

"Right. Till then!" I hung up.

I stood in front of the gate wondering what to do next. The fence seemed to have grown two or three feet taller since the night before. I despaired of seeing anyone who would be willing to give me the gate's code or let me inside. I hadn't seen more than three or four people since I'd arrived at the marina. And one of them had been Patterson, who didn't count.

I took a closer look at the gate, and the lock. It appeared to be very secure. Unless you had the code, you weren't going through that gate; that much was clear.

The sound of a car engine in the distance broke the silence. In a moment, a pair of headlights illuminated the road that ran past the marina. Someone was coming! What were the chances they would be coming to this gate? There had to be at least three or four others at intervals along the waterway.

I said a little prayer, not that I expected divine intervention and assistance in committing an illegal act. That seemed out of the range of the possible, and audacious besides. It just made me feel better to have someone else involved, even at this late date. I was beginning to wonder if I could handle the assignment alone. *Hey Sam*, I said to myself, *you have NO choice. You will handle the assignment, and you will succeed!* It's called self-talk, and in some circles it's well accepted as a behavior modification technique or a way of motivating oneself. In others, it will get you locked up.

Chapter Fifteen

The car pulled into the parking lot and stopped not far from the van. I had worked out earlier just how I would handle the scenario if I got an opportunity to request assistance from a passerby. I put my plan into action. Staggering in the direction of the car, which had now come to a stop, I hoped the car's occupants would turn out to be a couple. A couple might be more sympathetic to my plight.

"Excuse me!" I called out. A man and a woman, a little older than me, got out of the car. They didn't hear me at first, so I called out again.

"Hello, can you help me?" I hiccuped loudly.

This time they heard me and turned to see where my voice was coming from. I staggered toward them, giving a very convincing imitation of a lady who's imbibed one too many martinis. I've certainly seen enough people in that condition to be able to play the part well enough to fool most people.

"Hey, how are you?" I asked, putting a slur in my voice.

"Better than you, from the looks of it," the man replied, his tone smug and superior.

"You see, what happened is my boyfriend and I had a little fight. He left me at the bar and came back to the boat. I want to kiss and make up. But I forgot the code to unlock the gate. Can you help me?" I asked pitifully, thankful that none of my friends could see me playing the helpless female. It was not a role I relished.

"I don't know." He hesitated, so I seized the opportunity to sidle up to him.

"Frank, let's go," the woman said impatiently, tapping her fingers on his arm.

"Frank, come on, be a sport," I said in my sexiest voice. "If *you* had a fight with *your* lady, wouldn't you want someone to help her so *you* could kiss and make up?" I asked.

"Sure, I guess so. So where's your boyfriend?" he asked.

"Down there." I pointed down to the jetty where the sailboat was moored. "Can you open the gate for me?"

"I'm not sure. Our boat is moored at a different

dock. I'll try, but I'm not sure if the codes are all the same."

"Frank, come on," the woman whined.

"Just a minute, for Heaven's sake. I'll be there in a minute," he said impatiently, turning back to me with a grin.

Now Frank *really* wanted to help me. He was showing signs of wanting to dump his lady and come partying with me. I had to discourage that.

"My boyfriend is big and mean. If I don't get down to that boat in a hurry, he's going to feed me to the fishes." I laid it on thick.

"Okay, I'll try the gate for you. But if my code doesn't work, I can't help you." He went to the gate and punched in four numbers, then pulled on the gate.

I held my breath.

The gate creaked and swung open.

Thank God. "Thanks, Frankie. I'm forever in your debt," I said, giving him a wink.

"Hey, if it doesn't work out with your mean old man, come and see me," Frank called out, as he hurried after his lady friend.

"Sure, Frank." In your dreams, buddy.

As soon as Frank and his lady were out of sight, I slipped inside the gate and closed it behind me. I made my way slowly down the ramp onto the jetty, trying not to make it creak. The jetty moved and swayed with the water, and I swayed with it, taking a moment to get my sea legs. I looked around.

Most of the boats were dark; only the *Blondie* at the end of the dock, and one or two others, were lit up. Lucky for me there was a moon. It wasn't full, but it threw enough light that I could walk along the dock without tripping over the assortment of crabbing nets and fishing gear that people had left scattered across it.

When I finally arrived at the end of the dock, in front of Patterson's sailboat, I stopped and studied it for a moment while trying to decide on my next move. Now that I was there in front of the boat, with May so close, I began to get nervous.

What would Blondie do when she realized that I was there to set May free? She hadn't left with Patterson, so she was obviously still on board. She wouldn't relinquish their captive easily. I must admit, I was pleased to be dealing with her rather than Patterson. He packed a gun; he'd already pulled it on me once. I didn't want to go through that again.

I hadn't really decided on an approach, relying on events to direct the action. My plan was to do a little reconnaissance, check out the lay of the land, or should I say sea, and wait to see what developed.

I walked up the ramp onto the sailboat's deck and peered in the window of the cabin. No one was visible. Where was Blondie, and what was she up to? Was she hiding along with May, so that she wouldn't have to worry about being seen accidentally? Or were they sleeping, resting up for the impending voyage southward?

I tried the door, but of course it was locked. I looked in the window again. Still no sign of life. I pushed on the door once more, to make sure it was securely caught. I was just beginning to think that I might have to look for something to use to pry it open, when suddenly I felt the jab of a cold, hard object between my shoulder blades. Startled, I turned quickly and found myself staring down the barrel of yet another gun.

Not Blondie too, I thought!

Now, granted, it wasn't the same kind of gun as Patterson's, to be sure. It was a cute, little feminine gun, much smaller than his, with a pretty mother of pearl handle that glittered in the moonlight. Don't ask me what kind or caliber it was, because I have no idea. All I know is they all look lethal to me.

"Go on in, I've been expecting you," Blondie said. She used a key on the door and pushed it open.

"How so?" I asked. Darn it all! I hated being predictable. How had she managed to sneak up on me without my hearing her?

"Well, not you specifically, but someone. I told Bobby, 'They're not going to let you just waltz away with the money and the woman. They're going to want her back.' "

"You were right, Blondie. We do want her back.

Where is she?" Her only answer was an angry gesture toward the open door.

After obeying her terse order to enter the boat's cabin, I frantically scanned it for a clue as to where May might be hidden. I could see nothing other than another door at the far end of the room. There must be a second room beyond this one, and she must be hidden in it.

"Never mind," Blondie said.

"Hey, what's your name anyway? I can't keep calling you Blondie," I said, trying to distract her so that I could make a grab for the gun.

"My name is Sharon. But you can call me Mrs. Patterson."

"Bob's wife. Interesting," I said. "So what about his lady friend, Mary?"

"What are you talking about?" Her head snapped up and she gave me a fierce look. "If you think that nonsense is going to work with me, you've got another think coming. That's the oldest trick in the book."

"Hey, it's no bull. Didn't you know Bobby baby's been living with a woman in Burnaby? The have a cute little lovenest. She thinks he's going to marry *her*."

"Well, he can't, 'cuz he's already married, so shut up and get over there." She jabbed me with the gun, and pointed to the bench along the port side of the cabin.

I obliged. But reluctantly. If there's one thing I hate, it's being jabbed with a gun. It's enough to get me really steaming mad. I watched for an opportunity to get the upper hand, knowing that I had to proceed carefully or endanger both May and myself.

"Actually I met Bobby's girlfriend the other day. She's real nice. I think she's a little younger than you. Nice figure too. And no wrinkles. Not yet, anyway. I'll bet you got yours worrying about Bobby while he was behind bars," I said casually.

"Whatever," she said, but she was beginning to see red. Her mouth was set in a pout and frown lines furrowed her brow.

I pressed the point. "I'll bet you didn't know Mary was visiting him in prison. So you didn't have to worry about him being lonely. What do you think made Bobby choose a life of crime anyway? Did he have an unhappy childhood, or was it the stress of living with you?" I laid it on real thick.

"You know, now that I think of it, Bobby has been acting strangely lately." Blondie fumed as she started pacing the room, "There was that time a woman called him and left a message on his machine. That low down, good for nothing—"

I made my move in the split second when her back was turned slightly. Lunging toward her, I caught her around the waist. The gun went off, popping like a Fourth of July firecracker and startling both of us. We both went down with a thud, me on top of her. She hit her head on the bench on the opposite side of the cabin and crumpled in a heap under me. Knocked her right out!

I got up and dusted myself off, just like a hero in a cowboy flick. Feeling mighty pleased with myself, I looked around for some rope to tie her up. There was a storage locker under the seat of the bench and inside it a plastic buoy, the kind you throw to someone in the water when you want to play *ring around the body*. I quickly located a paring knife in the galley and cut the rope off the giant lifesaver, tying Blondie's hands and feet. She was lying peacefully, breathing quietly as if in a deep sleep.

Once I had her immobilized, I began to look for May. I found her bound and gagged and lying on a bunk bed in the forward cabin. She had heard us tussling, I guess, and was squirming, trying to free her hands. I untied the gag and used the paring knife to cut her loose, a far better use for it than peeling potatoes, I might add.

"Sam, I'm so glad to see you." She sat up, rubbing her wrists and moving her arms and legs gingerly to get the circulation going.

"Me too." I hugged her. "Are you all right?"

"I'm okay, a little battered and bruised but they didn't hurt me really. Just pushed me around a little. How's Richard? He must be beside himself."

"Now that you're safe, he'll be just fine. Hey, that reminds me, I have to call Fraser and let him know you're okay. What time is it?" I looked at my watch. It was almost one o'clock. Just about time for the meeting. "Let's get back to the car and out of here. Then I'll call and report in."

Chapter Sixteen

I never dreamt that May and I would have even more trouble getting out of the marina gate than I had getting in. How was I to know that you needed the code on both sides of the fence? I guess you could call it poor planning on my part, if you wanted to hurt my feelings.

All I know is, after we left the boat, I expected it to be clear sailing, but alas, it was not to be. We stole along the jetty and climbed the ramp, only to be stopped short by the locked gate.

We sat there in the dark waiting for someone to come along and open it. While we waited, May told me the story of how Patterson had caught up to her in the parking lot of the Safeway in New Westminster, taken her at gunpoint to Mary Lucas's apartment, tied her up, and stuck her in the closet. Mary had not been there. Before Mary had come home, he had moved her down to Point Roberts to the boat, but not before she managed to get her hands free and leave a note and her purse behind, pulling the coats down off their hangers to cover it up. She didn't really think anyone would find it. It was a long shot. She never saw Mary, but heard Patterson talking to her on the phone. She had heard him mention the boat, the *Blondie*, to her. It was by no means certain that he would be taking her there, May said, but she took a chance and wrote in the notebook, *Find Blondie*. Thank goodness we had been able to figure it out, with Mary's help.

Finally after over an hour of waiting, a car pulled into the parking lot and a man came up to the gate. He pressed the numbers on the keypad and came through the gate. When he saw us on the other side he looked at us strangely, but didn't protest when I grabbed the gate and held it open. Once he had passed through, we went out and shut it behind us.

I settled May in the van, and prepared to head toward the border. But before I started the engine, it dawned on me that I had neglected to call Fraser. He would be wondering if something had gone wrong. And I wanted to find out what was happening at the Park.

I punched in his cell phone number and waited while it rang, once, twice, three times. No answer.

Finally a recorded voice came on the line. "*The customer you are dialing is temporarily unavailable or out of the service area.*" What the heck?

I called Richard's place to talk to Martha. At least she answered, and on the first ring.

"Martha, Sam here. Have you heard from the others?"

"Not a word. I was beginning to get worried. Where are you?"

"I'm at the marina and I've got May. She's fine. If Fraser calls in, you can tell him she's okay. I'm heading back into town. I'll call again a little later."

"Okay. Take care."

I hung up and started the car. I told May about Richard and Fraser having a rendezvous at the Park with Patterson. She insisted we go there; she wanted to see Richard as soon as possible. I have to admit I didn't really try to dissuade her, since I was curious about what was happening and why I couldn't reach Fraser on his phone. Perhaps it would have been much better if we had just planned to do the smart thing and go to Richard's to wait for the others, but that would have been much too logical and safe—two words that don't figure much in my vocabulary or my behavior. In the end it didn't really make a difference what we planned. The decision was taken out of our hands, in a manner of speaking.

The border crossing was uneventful. The Canadian customs official was polite but uninterested in two slightly bedraggled women crossing into Canada late at night. He probably thought we'd been at the bingo hall.

Now, as a person goes through the border into Canada, the road turns around the building and joins with the southbound lane to become 56th, a two-way street. As I turned the van around the building, what I saw almost made me drive into the cement curbing surrounding it. There was Patterson's Ford heading south, back to the Point. He was sitting in line, one or two cars in front of him, waiting to go through the American customs.

At about the same time I spotted him, he eye-balled me, and May. The look on his face was price-less. I don't know which of us was more shocked.

May recognized the Ford, and she started to scream, making me wonder if she'd been telling the truth about not having been mistreated while in Patterson's company. I patted her arm and said, "There, there" while maneuvering into the driving lane to head North. What the heck was Patterson doing back at the Point? It was only around two. He should have been at Central Park, or at least just beginning his trip back to the Point.

I stepped on the gas, trying to get a jump on Patterson in the event he made a move to follow us. May undid her seatbelt and turned around in her seat, watching the Ford.

"He's turning down that little road before the border and going around the Canadian customs building. I think he's coming after us," she warned.

"Sit down and buckle up," I said. "I don't know what the heck he's doing back there, but I'm not going to hang around to find out. Let's see how fast we can get out of here." I floored the gas pedal and the van jumped ahead, but this momentum didn't last for long.

"Let's see if we can pick up a police escort," I said to May, thinking that if I sped through town, some obliging police cruiser might see me and pull me over. I should have known better. Where *are* the boys in uniform when you need them?

May ignored my request to fasten her seatbelt. She was kneeling on the seat beside me, watching out the back window and reporting on Patterson's location as we sped down the long hill into Tsawwassen, through a series of lights, and toward the highway into town.

"He's about three cars behind us. He's really tailgating the car in front of him trying to find an opportunity to pass. Thank goodness there's some traffic or he'd be right on our tail."

I glanced in the rear view mirror to see if I could spot the Ford. I could just barely make it out in the distance. For the moment we were safe, but once we both reached the highway, look out. I put the *pedal to the metal*, as the saying goes, but how much can you ask of an old beat-up VW van? She didn't have a lot of power to give. I was proud of her though; she gave it all she had and then some.

As I was driving, I was trying to figure out what to do next to get us out of this mess. It seemed to me that our destination should still be Central Park. I had no idea what had gone wrong. Why was Patterson not there with the others? Whatever the reason, since that was where the cops were, as well as Fraser and Richard, I could think of no better place to lead him than right into their trap.

If only I could stay enough ahead of him to arrive even a minute or so before he did, I thought, I'd be able to warn the rest of the gang of his impending arrival. Dream on, Sam. One look in the rearview mirror made me realize it was going to be all I could do to stay ahead of him at all. He was now only two cars behind, having passed one of the vehicles as soon as we hit the highway. I decided to take the Knight Street Bridge, and go straight up Knight to 49th, then along 49th until it became Imperial at Boundary Road.

I could credit myself with quick thinking, at least, since I was plotting my route, destination, and possible evasive action simultaneously. May was watching our rear and hollering progress reports every mile or two. I have to give her her due as well. She's one spunky lady.

"Hang on, May, here we go," I said, almost en-

joying my licence to speed. I didn't care how fast I
went or who saw me. In fact, I would have been
delighted to see a police cruiser on the roadside. The
only thing I feared was photo radar. It clocked you
and spat out tickets without offering any help for
your troubles. I was counting on the late hour to
give me relatively clear passage. I didn't want to
cause an accident.

Patterson was persistent, but he couldn't seem to
get past the couple of cars between us. I didn't even
try to duck down a side street or take the corners at
breakneck speed. I could see no point. I didn't want
to lose him. I wanted him to follow us to the Park;
not to catch us before then, mind you; just to stick
with us until we reached help.

Once I got onto 49th Avenue, I knew I was going
to make my destination without Patterson catching
up. What a relief! My father would never have for-
given me if I rescued May only to get her killed or
maimed by my reckless driving, or by Patterson and
his bullets connecting with us.

To say that our arrival at the park was welcomed
would be a slight exaggeration of the sentiments
expressed by Richard and Fraser. Of course there
was a touching reunion between Richard and May
with tears all round. Even my eyes were runny, but
I put it down to the wind blowing dust into my eyes.

I grabbed hold of Fraser's arm and pulled him off

to one side. He seemed intent on lecturing me about having brought May to the park. But I knew we only had a matter of a minute or two until Patterson arrived and no time to conduct a postmortem on my decision.

Patterson had been close on my tail all through town. Just before the park, I had seen him get caught by a red light when I squeaked through on the yellow. I had to talk fast.

"Patterson's on his way," I said, interrupting Fraser. "I don't know why, but he was heading back to the Point and spotted us at the border. What happened?" I asked.

"He never showed up here," Fraser said. "I don't know whether he drove up, spotted the police and got cold feet, or what happened, but we waited for ages and he never showed. The police packed up and went home."

"You mean they're not here?" I yelled, gesturing toward the public facilities.

"No, we're all alone."

"Oh my God. He'll be here any second. He was right behind us all the way from the border. What are we going to do?" I was jumping up and down at that point, frantic to figure out something before Patterson arrived.

"Stay calm, Sam," Fraser said, grabbing my arm and holding me still. "Remember, we've got the money. I knew it would come in handy. I'll go and get it out of the car. You take May, and go and hide in the washroom. I'll let Richard know what's up." Fraser reached behind his back and pulled a gun out of his waistband, taking off the safety and putting the gun in his jacket pocket.

"Go on, Sam, we don't have any time to lose." He pushed me forward.

I ran over to May, told her to follow me, and led her to the cement building on the edge of the clearing. From our vantage point, we could see Fraser gesturing toward his car, then running over and opening the trunk. Richard was still standing in the clearing, waiting for Patterson, I guessed.

As soon as I had the presence of mind, I punched in Richard's home phone number and got hold of Martha.

"Martha, I don't have time to talk. Call the police; you've got the number Fraser gave you. Tell them to come back to Central Park. Tell them Patterson's on his way here. Tell them we got May out safely."

"What's going on?"

"I can't explain now; I'll call back once things calm down." I hung up.

From the window of the washroom, I could see car lights approaching the corner. The vehicle pulled over and stopped. The lights went out, and the scene went black again. There was a quick flash of light from the trees behind Richard. That must be Fraser signaling to Richard to let him know he was in position.

"Howell, you double-crossed me," Patterson growled as he approached the spot where Richard was waiting. Patterson had his gun cocked and pointed straight at Richard.

"No, I didn't. I'm here, and so is the money. You didn't think I was going to let you hold May after you got the money, did you? That would have been just plain foolish."

"I thought I told you no police," Patterson insisted.

Richard didn't answer. I couldn't help but wonder where he was getting his nerve. This was a side of my father I had never seen before. Perhaps the side that had got him into trouble when he and my mother had separated so many years before. I was ridiculously proud of the way he was standing his ground against Patterson, who had advanced to within a few feet of him and still had the gun trained on him.

"Let's see the money."

"If you want it, come and get it," Richard replied in an offhand way that made my blood run cold. What was he up to?

Just give him the money and let him go, I thought, willing my father to receive my telepathic message and back off. No such luck.

"Don't try anything funny," Patterson growled.

"Believe me, I don't find this situation the least bit funny," Richard replied.

Patterson bent over and reached out to pick up the duffel bag. For an instant, his gun was no longer trained on Richard. All of a sudden it was as if I knew exactly what was going to happen next, but was powerless to prevent it.

Richard pulled a gun out of his pocket and pointed it right at Patterson.

"Back off, Patterson," he hollered.

Patterson, who you would have thought would have dropped his gun, instead swung his arm up and fired.

Two more shots rang out almost simultaneously. I saw Richard slump to the ground, but not before Patterson, who fell hard, landing on top of the duffel bag full of money.

Sirens screamed in the distance, and I cursed them. What had taken them so long?

May cried out when she saw Richard fall. She sprinted across the clearing and knelt down to gather him in her arms. He moaned and held his arm. Thank goodness! He appeared to be only slightly injured.

Fraser reached Richard about the same time as May, and when he saw that Richard's arm was only grazed by Patterson's bullet, he turned his attention on Patterson who was stirring slightly. Patterson made a move to sit up, then fell over again.

Fraser must have figured that Patterson was on his last legs, as he left him and went back over to Richard to help him up.

From my vantage point, I could see everyone clearly. Intent on helping Richard and May, Fraser was crouched over Richard with his back to Patterson.

All at once Patterson made one final attempt to get up on his feet. Oh no! Where was his gun? I came racing out of the washroom, hollering at Fraser to watch out.

I must say Fraser's reflexes were excellent. He responded instantly by turning and pointing his gun at Patterson. He was just in time to see Patterson dragging himself upright. When Patterson saw Fraser take aim, he just gave up. Holding his stomach, he fell down hard and for the last time.

I was willing to bet he had been trying to make it to his car and back across the border to Blondie and the sailboat. But it wasn't meant to be; he had breathed his last breath.

Four police cars converged on the Park. As soon as we explained the situation, two of them went back to the station while the other two remained behind to help us and to secure the crime scene.

Another siren screamed toward us, and I realized gratefully that someone had had the presence of mind to call 911 for an ambulance for Richard. It was not me. My legs finally gave way, and I slid down into a heap on the ground. And that's where Fraser found me, when he bothered to come looking.

Epilogue

Patterson was pronounced dead at the scene. He never made it back to his wife and his sailboat, *The Blondie*.

The police obtained the assistance of the Whatcom County Sheriff's office to pick up Sharon Patterson. She is currently cooling her heels in a jail cell in Bellingham, while the Canadian government prepares extradition papers.

May rode to the hospital in the ambulance with Richard. She refused to be separated from him, ever again. That's what she said.

Fraser insisted I leave the van parked on Imperial, at the entrance to Central Park. He personally escorted me to his car, half-carrying half-walking me there. He was most solicitous, and though I'm one of those thoroughly modern, independent women most of the time, I admit I enjoyed being pampered, if only for a little while. I sat in the car while he spoke to the police, who were cleaning up the crime scene. Then he took me home.

Poor Martha. No one had thought to call her back since my frantic phone call asking her to contact the police. She was almost beside herself. It took us the rest of the night to fill her in on what had happened, each of us piecing it together for the other right up to the conclusion.

I myself paid a visit to Mary Lucas. I didn't want her to find out about Patterson's death through the media. It turned out she had no idea either that Patterson was married or that he had kidnapped May and had been holding her to force Richard to give him $250,000. To tell you the truth, I think she was relieved that she wouldn't have him around anymore, though I'm sure she would have preferred to see him locked up again, rather than six feet under.

As for Fraser and me, well, let's just say adversity brought us closer. After we finished yelling at one another for our mutual bungling of the affair, we agreed that it didn't really matter since May was safe and sound and Patterson gone to his reward, or punishment. We settled into a nice routine that had me cooking, yes I said cooking, dinner for him regularly and him reciprocating. We were taking it slowly. I still hadn't let him read my books.

Mimi had grown quite fond of Fraser; it was as though she remembered their abrupt introduction at the doggie social club on Dallas Drive. We often go to the area. Fraser is trying, so far in vain, to teach Mimi to fetch. Talk about Mission Impossible!

You know, I *had* only been joking about wanting to keep the money from the robbery. I had no idea there was a reward for its safe return to the bank. But when the dust settled, I got a tidy little sum, enough to allow me to go out and book a plane ticket to France. The only problem is that I haven't been able to get hold of Gabby since she went to Paris with Jean-Claude. I've sent repeated e-mail, to no avail. I'm beginning to get worried. So I'm leaving next week. Going to find out for myself just what that Frenchman is up to. No good, I'm sure.